Plainsong

Plainsong

a novel

Nancy Huston

STEERFORTH PRESS
SOUTH ROYALTON, VERMONT

For information about permission to reproduce
selections from this book, write to:
Steerforth Press L.C., P.O. Box 70,
South Royalton, Vermont 05068

Library of Congress Cataloging-in-Publication Data

Huston, Nancy, 1953–
[Cantique des plaines. English]
Plainsong : a novel / Nancy Huston.
p. cm.
ISBN 1-58642-014-3 (alk. paper)
I. Title.
PQ3919.2.H87 C3613 2001
843'.914—dc21

2001017002

FIRST STEERFORTH EDITION

For the Fish

Then you ain't saved?

– Flannery O'Connor
from "Good Country People"

And here is how I visualize the moment of your death: a falling away a draining and receding and lightening and melting and sliding of the world like the gradual disappearance of snow in the forest, or like colours slowly spilling outside the frame and leaving nothing on the canvas, while in the meantime your limbs grew numb and leaden, becoming one with the mattress, the floor, the earth, even your rage turning to froth and its millions of bubbles bursting as your mind sank deeper and deeper into matter . . . I see a long highway curving across the plain and the sun beating down on it, beating you down into the asphalt, the crushed rock and tar — you're part of that road now Paddon, that endless grey ribbon of an idea about going somewhere — lying flat yes flattened at last into the plain from which you'd struggled to arise — a faintly perceptible scar on its surface. Finally the draining and falling and spilling away reached your face, the weight pushed against your features dragging them downward and the very last thing registered by your brain before it succumbed to the bulldozer of asphalt numbness was Grandma's voice whispering *Forgive us our trespasses.*

Then nothing.

I could not, would not attend your funeral, I preferred to sit here all these miles away and close my eyes and try to see . . . *Hit the road, Jack* . . . Yes my darling Grandad after all these years — you were pretty much as old as the century, and this century is about as old as a century can get — you've finally hit the road. No last will and testament, Mother informed me over the telephone, since your earthly possessions were scarcely worth a passing mention. Grandma will probably keep your piano as it makes an excellent display case for her knick-knacks cut-glass decanters and English porcelain statues of red-lipped children hugging dogs, their hair tousled by the wind, but she will no doubt give your clothing away to the Salvation Army — that's the proper thing to do — fold up her deceased husband's thick flannel shirts and his long underwear gone off-white from manic washing and the two or three pairs of pants that held his poor sad genitals for so many useless years and stack them in a cardboard box and donate them to charity; perhaps next year she will recognize them on a drunken Indian lying in a stinking heap over on Eighth Avenue and feel a little glow of goodness at the centre of her heart...

O breather into man of breath O holder of the keys of death O giver of the life within Save us from death the death of sin That body soul and spirit be For ever living unto thee — May he rest in peace. The hymn-book is snapped shut by hairy plump white hands and the skinny straggle of mourners stands there glancing around and hesitating, wondering if they may move now, no not yet, not yet, yes now, their feet begin to shift, they are shod with synthetic boots or plastic galoshes or leatherette sensible shoes, they move away stiff and stodgy from the edge of the abyss. All I can see for now are the hands and the feet . . . It is barely spring a chilly morning in early spring, early spring in these latitudes is late in the month of April, clumps of snow are still banked against some of the gravestones and the ground must have been hard to dig but now the grave has been emptied of hard mud and filled with

Paddon and hard mud and now it is over. I can't quite see the faces yet but I'm beginning to see the clothes, dark in honour of the occasion and purchased on the sole basis of the fact they don't need ironing. The bodies: many of them are overweight, impeded by unsightly rolls of flesh around the waist and knees and ankles, those that are not overweight are collapsed inwards hunched or shrivelled — sad bodies on the whole with awkward arms, hands shaking one another flaccidly and falling back to sides, heads and tongues wagging dutifully though there is nothing much to say, basically there is never anything much to say but especially in this case given the fact that Paddon was nigh on ninety and all of us have to go someday and indeed most of us have gone already and all we can do is hope that God sees fit to call us back to His side as peacefully as he did Paddon, and well my dear we should be going shouldn't we it wouldn't do to catch cold would it.

The heads move back and forth or up and down making the jowls jiggle slightly and if I concentrate very hard I can distinguish blue veins through the reddish pink skin, the women are wearing little or no make-up and their stockings are thick beige rayon rather than sheer risqué nylon, their gloves are sensible also and they never get mislaid, everyone virtually without exception is wearing glasses, the men's hair is grey or white and the women's is pale blue, the men cut theirs short and part it neatly on one side if they have anything left to part, the women go once a fortnight to have theirs crimped and primped into arrested blue waves, their purses tend to match their shoes, the colours are navy blue or black or brown because these go well with everything and don't show dirt as quickly as lighter tones, their coats are warm, selected to endure through one after another of these harsh everlasting winters. No one laughs of course but then neither does anyone shed tears — these people have spent their lives scouring spontaneity from their souls, the single and conspicuous exception is Paddon's sister Elizabeth, kneeling in the mud and snow at the foot of the grave, passionately moving her lips with eyes closed and tears streaming down her cheeks, crossing herself ecstatically again and again but then everyone knows she's an eccentric, too many years in the tropics and a Catholic to boot, the minister is already unlocking his car door and the mourners are murmuring that they really should be getting home too, though most of them are elderly and long retired except your own children of course who aren't that young anymore themselves, and as for your widow Karen she is bravely holding her head up standing tall and straight next to her tall straight daughter my mother Ruthie and murmuring the Lord's Prayer for the millionth time in her life between lips whitened blue by the cold; she is just now getting to the part about *Lead us not into temptation.*

Ah but wouldn't it be terrific I can't help thinking if this grey and grimly smiling lady could allow herself to be led into temptation for a change — what would it be? A rhumba a tango a cha-cha-cha a glass of Cuban rum an amber-skinned stranger stinging ember eyes into her? What is she worried about now that she's almost home free what could possibly happen to her at eighty-odd what is the temptation? Cheating at bridge? Wearing the same cotton drawers three days in a row because she didn't feel like washing them after two? Stealing an extra can of dog food from the supermarket for her fox terrier? Elizabeth gets to her feet at last, crosses herself one more time *in the name of the Father the Son and the Holy Ghost Amen* and, cheeks glistening with joyful tears and overcoat dripping with slush, rejoins Karen her sister-in-law. The two elderly women embrace while the younger older woman Ruthie waits for them to stop. Then they all drive away smoothly in their heated expensive cars — these are not rich people but they have taken the art of pinching pennies seriously for decades and know how essential it is to have a good car hereabouts so they buy a new one every two or three years in more or less the same hues as the ladies' shoes and for the same reasons — back to their medium-sized houses whose mortgages are now fully paid off so they don't have to worry about *that* anymore, and having locked their car doors and their garage doors they unlock their front doors or their side doors and remove their rubber boots or galoshes if they were wearing them or, if not, wipe their shoes carefully on Welcome mats purchased through the Eaton's mail-order catalogue and sit down on upholstered chesterfields with doilies on the arms and backs and look calmly at the television or speak politely to one other or turn the pages of a magazine while they wait for it to be time for lunch.

Grandma mailed me a thick outspilling envelope labelled firmly in her hand *P's Book* and filled with ancient pages written in your hand, your many hands, some rollicking others wretched and others weary — oh Paddon I can still see those hands of yours, thick strong fingers tamping tobacco or playing piano, amazingly nimble despite age and arthritis, making tunes appear and go lilting sideways into other tunes, teaching me how to put my thumb under my second and third fingers quick as a wink, twisting pipe-cleaners into animals, chucking me under the chin good night — okay so now it's mine. Now the responsibility is mine.

No, I haven't forgotten my promise. You must have thought I had. I know you remembered it to the end, though two decades have gone by without our so much as alluding to it once.

Why me, Grandad?

Even when I was tiny you stood me between your thighs and took my questions seriously, talked to me of shooting stars and hobgoblins, explained the newspaper to me from current events to cartoons, looked at me with your sad eyes and laughed at every single one of my jokes.

When I was six you lifted me next to you on the piano bench and told me about Scarlatti's cat. One day, you explained, Scarlatti's cat marched delicately across the keyboard, setting its paws down precisely and at random, every five semitones or so, and the composer made a fugue of the melody thus produced. That, you told me, is love.

Listen — one note after the other, going up. Slow strange solitary notes. A lot of flats. A lot of black notes. One, one, one, one, one, one — going up. Listen — in an inimitably minor key. You walked across the keyboard of the century, Paddon, trying to watch where you were going, and you failed. Listen to the notes. Black and white notes played out virtually at random. But a lot of flats. A lot of accidentals. You kept on waiting for Scarlatti to intervene, didn't you? You couldn't believe there was no Scarlatti, there would never be any Scarlatti. You would rather have smashed the piano to smithereens than accept the idea that no Scarlatti would come, ever, to build a fugue around your mournful melody. All you managed to do was bloody up some of the notes.

When I was eight you took an atlas down from the shelf, opened it to the map of Alberta and taught me to hear the different melodies playing in the names of your world, a structure which had been shakily erected on three unequal columns.

Tawatinaw	Belly River	Lac La Nonne
Nemiskam	Grassy Lake	Vegreville
Wetaskiwin	Winnifred	Bellevue
Athabasca	Bad Heart	Balzac
Chipewyan	Heath	Lac La Biche
Otauwau River	Drumheller	Brousseau
Keoma	Iron Springs	Quatre Fourches
Waskatenau	Entwistle	Lacombe
Ponoka	Lesser Slave Lake	Joussard
Kapasiwin River	Saddle	Embarras Portage
	Fort McMurray	Grande Prairie
	Enchant	Rivière Qui Barre
	Entrance	
	Entice	
	Bindloss	
	Dunvegan	
	Swan Hills	
	Peace River	
	Iddesleigh	
	Sedalia	
	Fawcett	
	Driftpile	
	Hotchkiss	
	Mirror	
	Crooked Creek	
	Killam	
	Hardisty	
	Pollockville	
	Didsbury	

It went on and on. Some of the names set me dreaming. Peace River, Enchant. Peace River, Enchant. Oh . . . I remember too how much you despised that song *This Land Is Your Land*, how you refused to allow it to be sung within your earshot. The time I came home from summer camp with those words on my lips was the one and only time you aimed your ire at me — such beautiful words I thought — we'd been singing them in harmony night after night around the campfire then all the way back to Calgary on the bus — *As I was walking that ribbon of highway I saw above me that endless skyway I saw below me that golden valley This land was made for you and me* — and hearing me you harrumphed and muttered something like Cut the fucking crap, and Grandma pulled you away and shushed and fussed and said Paddon for Heaven's sake she can't be expected to understand, it's just a song she learned at camp, and meanwhile, filthy from a week of learning to follow trails through the woods and recognize stars and bird-calls and sleep in a tent, a week of pretending to be an Indian in my group of rosy-cheeked blue-uniformed blonde-pigtailed Girl Guides called the Sarcees, I had gone up to my room and thrown myself fully dressed on the sparkling white coverlet and cried myself to sleep.

And yet Paddon, incomprehensibly to me coming from the East, you loved this land, loved its emptiness its hugeness its open flatness the exciting biting cold the white snow in sun that hurt your eyes the forthright way the air attacked your cheekbones chin and fingers, the merciless summer sun that made the train-tracks flash and the air above the wheatfields shimmer the purple storm-clouds piled on the horizon trying to look like mountains while the real mountains sat there, inimitable, a scant eighty miles away. Alberta and Montana,

8

you told me, were arbitrarily different names for what had always been the same place, and the feverish staking-out of the forty-ninth parallel, followed by a pompous marquis' dedication of seventeen million acres of prairie land to some priggish Victorian princess who had never left the British Isles, did not change the true soul of the place one whit: this was Big Sky country.

Hit the Road Jack — You never did manage to hit the road, Paddon. Never once left the confines of your province. And now your own bones are in the Alberta ground.

This land is my land at long last.

I'm trying to read the manuscript. In the last — no, next-to-last — years of your life you scribbled and scratched and scraped away at the versions that had been sketched out in the fifties. You still wanted to get something across but it was so far down, so hemmed in by continual quellings and qualifications, that even its essential shape is now impossible to guess at. Most of the manuscript pages are indecipherable. There are fifty tentative titles on the title page, the last the most tentative of all: *The Time Being*. Of the several hundred sheets of mangled foolscap, only a few paragraphs emerge unscathed.

> *The words go forward. Language unfolds in time. It can slow time down, it can hold — hold — hold the tick of seconds, hover, pretend to freeze, and point to its own miraculous suspension, but it cannot make time go backwards. There is no reverse gear to the vehicle. Language plunges headlong into the future. Words must be pronounced, their pronunciation takes time, and even were we to render them meaningless by pronouncing them*

9

backwards they would still take time except that it would be wasted time . . . even more wasted than usual.

When I read that yesterday afternoon, I felt like giving up once and for all. The fear that's always haunted me came back, larger than life now that you've passed away — that if I get too close to you you'll infect me with your despair. I lay down on my bed and stared at the ceiling until the flashing lights from the Café Expresso across the street began to chase each other around the walls of my room. Then I got up, turned on my desk lamp and read for the rest of the night. This is one of the longest passages I was able to piece together more or less coherently:

> *. . . night after night, time would behave unspeakably. I'd be fishing on the pier at the pond near Uncle Jake's as I had every summer of my boyhood. I'd be sitting there — and suddenly, absolutely nothing would happen. The indifferent, irregular unfolding of events would simply cease. No dragonfly would alight on the pier, no fish would leap above the surface of the pond, no leafy branch would rustle in the breeze, no mosquito would settle slyly into the sweaty backs of my knees, no daisy or dandelion would nod its head — nothing. All events would simply not take place. And then — but what was the nature of this then? what could possibly be the meaning of sequence in a universe of suspended time? (this was the question that would make me sit bolt upright in bed or flail about desperately until Karen shook me awake) — then, everything would happen at once.*
>
> *All the possible events of the situation would occur in one fell swoop. All the clouds would rush across the sky, all the insects would alight on the pier, a host of mosquitoes would pump my blood in unison. Sequentiality had been destroyed. Things no longer happened in order, causes were no longer distinct from their effects, a sort of silent pandemonium had broken loose.*
>
> *These dreams I think date back to around '34 when my mother died, but all those years are a single . . .*

The passage grows illegible at this point, violently so. But after a few hours' muggy morning sleep, I think I finally see what it is I have to do. I'll need a lot of time and gall and imagination . . . and especially luck. My documentation is pretty paltry — but you'll help me, won't you, Paddon?

As a child you lived in the ranchlands southwest of Calgary, that much I know, near a town called Anton. I never met my great-grandmother Mildred but the photo album shows her to have belonged to the same physical type as your sister Elizabeth: broad-shouldered, flat-chested women who treated their bodies like powerful tanks or battleships, ate as though they were filling up on gas and oil, walked as though they were activating pistons, talked as though they were tapping out radio messages with no conceivable ambiguity at either end. I stare at the photographs, losing my gaze in the bony girth of these women's hips as they go about their girdled business, and wonder how the song of the intricate folds of flesh between their thighs could have been so effectively silenced.

What was it like to have a mother like that, Paddon?

———•—•———

Mildred was a ranch wife, one of those no-nonsense ladies from England who responded to the appeal for members of the fairer sex to come and join the go-West-young-men when they started getting lonely after a few years of roughing it on the frontier. She arrived just before the turn of the century at age twenty, brave because she knew the Injuns had been safely put away on reservations or enlisted as domestic help whose required uniform was not a starched white apron neatly tied around the waist

11

but a ball and chain neatly attached to the left foot. Yes by that time the prairies had been made empty — land, land, come and get it, millions of acres of land, no taxes, low fares, great topsoil, fantastic farming potential, new hard wheat, the last best West is going fast — and the land rush began, the goal being to replace the vanished buffalo with cows and the vanished Indians with cowboys as fast as possible, and the men poured in, the failures poured in, the criminals poured in, young and muscular, rough and rowdy, not particularly educated but proud of the way they held their liquor, especially compared with the Injuns, and glad of a new lease on life after having fucked up on the other side of the ocean. Your father came that way, one of the first, a stubborn Irish kid brought up in dirt poverty in England, leaping straight from bankruptcy in English dairy farming to hopes of gold galore in the Great North. Yes I see it now, I think that's how it must have happened: the Sterling brothers John and Jake came to Canada with visions of Dawson City dancing in their heads.

Who were these people Paddon, who were these one hundred thousand men with their handful of loose women and loose change that were prepared to slug and lug unwieldy bundles of food and belongings through twenty-four months and twenty-four hundred miles of physical torture, prepared to endure blizzards and chilblains, hunger and howling wind, scurvy and solitude, snow caked on eyelashes, what were these men Paddon, who was this father of yours drawn by a dream of sheer and shameless wallowing in wealth — it was he who had wheedled and pleaded, wasn't it, he who had dragged Jake into the plan, he who on a trip to London in July of '97 had heard the paper boys shouting themselves hoarse about a steamer recently arrived in Seattle bearing two tons my God two tons sweet bloomin' Christ two tons of Klondike gold, and though he could not read the papers he could eavesdrop in the pubs, and the fever caught him and flushed right through his eager scrawny soul and he grabbed his younger brother and infected him with it as best he could, and where oh where did they ever scrabble up the funds for the crossing, were they stowaways or did they hire out their wiry biceps, heaven knows, somehow they crossed the Atlantic then probably hopped a CP freight and after weeks of bone-jolting nerve-jarring travel in boxcars wound up in Edmonton where their troubles could begin.

He never told you this story Paddon, so you never told Ruthie and she never told me but I'm almost sure it happened and I sit here at my desk in a heated apartment, reading and musing and motionless hour after hour, trying to feel the lunge and desperation of those men. They were willing to plough through the hellchill for the promise of instant wealth in Dawson City: what they wanted was gold and what they hoped for was to come back with it but what awaited them was an out-and-out orgy of gamble and guzzle and grab. Dawson City was the uncharted frozen heart of Dante's inferno: its inhabitants were condemned to pure and purposeless pleasure for as long as they could pay. The rest of the world might toil in offices and rice fields, buy tickets to the opera or carve sacred ancestral masks, but up there, far above the Arctic Circle, human existence would be eternally confined to riotous celebration. Gold dust was the only legal tender and nugget necklaces the only jewels; the acting-out of fantasies was compulsory. All the accoutrements of civilization — Paris gowns, aged malt whisky, roulette wheels, cigars — were props for a savage theatre performance that went on day and night in the middle of nowhere. You paid to play and you paid to drink and you paid to dance and dally with the dames, you won you lost you won and lost again until you were quite spent, emptied of your last spurt of sperm, your last twinge of energy, your last fleck of gold.

The dream of gold burned behind your father's eyes all through the winter of '98, and Jake stayed dubiously but unflaggingly at his side as, along with a dozen other mackinawed and muklukked idiots rigged out in Komfortable Kostumes for the Klondyke by Larue & Picard, they straggled down or rather up the Skagway Trail. None of these people had ever been as gifted at planning as they were at dreaming; besides, the businessmen back in Edmonton had airily lied to them about the great northern trails which stayed open all winter long, there were no trails at all up here, it was as simple as that, no Indian in his right mind had ever attempted to cross these vast wastes in the short-day months and it was against their better judgement that a few of them, under the influence of fear or alcohol, grudgingly agreed to accompany the gold-diggers. But their atrociously slow progress grew even slower when the spring thaw came, the ice turned to swamp and the dogsleds were constantly getting stuck in the dense muskeg, so when in February supplies started running out and one of the men had to chop off his own gangrened foot your father and uncle got a bit nervous, and when in March men started shooting beaver, cutting the hair off them and boiling them to drink the liquor and chew the skins they got a bit disgusted, and when in April the Indian guides announced that their only hope for survival was to eat some of the dogs, and the oldest prospector having been informed that Dawson City was still fifteen hundred miles away blew out his brains they hastily conferred and decided to turn back.

No gold, no go — they hadn't even made it to the Arctic Circle! However as they slid back southwards towards spring they noticed along with many millions of mosquitoes that the land around them was extraordinarily fertile, and by the time their emaciated exhausted bodies reached the town of Peace River Junction everything was greening and growing, so as soon as they had stuffed enough stew into their stomachs to think straight they began concocting a new dream: farming up here together, wresting fame and fortune from this soil, founding a dynasty of wealthy Sterling homesteaders father to son.

Your mother arrived a year later, tall and tough and healthy; if she'd been frail and feminine she doubtless would not have needed to travel to the ends of the earth to find herself a mate.

I don't yet know exactly how they met but I know that the world in which they met was a world of madness, Paddon, a crazy-making world in which people were scattered through empty space and endless flatness, a house here and then nothing as far as the eye could see, a house there and then nothing nothing nothing. It was a world of solitude, unspeakable solitude and fear and hardship — perhaps no human community ever anywhere had been so primitive, each of its members eking out a subsistence in absolute isolation, unable to communicate with one another and preoccupied solely with forcing a living out of the land, their vocabulary and behaviour whittled down to bare necessities, food clothing work money money work clothing food, and their souls answerable only to God though what they meant by God was a dozen different things — they were Mennonites Hutterites Mormons Seventh Day Adventists Methodists Baptists Catholics and two or three godforsaken Jews. Here was a Finn and here a German and here a Dutchman and here a Swede, here was an Englishman and here a Pole, there a Ukrainian and over there a Frenchman of noble stock in flight from the rotting modern world. They brought their women with them or had them follow once the house was built, or else they advertised for strong young women to come over and join forces with them — and when the women came, leaving behind cities like Vienna where Schoenberg was putting the finishing touches on the dodecaphonic system, or Barcelona where Picasso was astounding his masters at the Academy, or Paris where Charcot was displaying to sober beard-stroking medical students his voluptuous white-gowned hysterics frozen in various erotic postures, leaving behind concert halls and cathedrals and café-theatres, intricate lace and sheeny sculpted furniture, when they disembarked after weeks of gruelling travel first by boat and then by train they found nothing, no neighbourhood no chitchat no exchanging recipes no gossiping about friends, nothing but the wild West, far wilder now than it had been a century before, wilder than the innermost reaches of Africa or the Amazon, a land full of emptiness and strange languages and hard hard hard work to be done.

Mildred sure knew how to work, didn't she? You've got to hand her that. Ferocious. She was at it from before dawn till after dusk, making her own bread with a special brown-sugar recipe that rose every time, churning butter with a vertical wood-on-wood thumping vengeance, whipping up batches of flapjacks or corn muffins at a moment's notice to feed twenty men on round-up day, sweeping clouds of dirt outside from the rough wooden floors, shovelling snow, knitting scarves and darning socks, scrubbing clothes on a corrugated board in a washtub and hanging them next to the stove, bathing you in the same tub with the stove door open, sticking washcloths down your ears and up your nose, Cleanliness is next to godliness and I will not put up with little boys who are dirty or lazy, do you hear? *Holy, Holy, Holy! Lord God Almighty! Early in the morning our song shall rise to thee* . . . Many of her favourite hymns harped on getting up early in the morning, which was something you detested.

Your father sang a song that started out the same way — *Early in the mornin' when the sun is risin' See the little engines all in a row See the little driver pull the little lever Choo-choo-choo and away we go Down by the Bay Where the watermelons grow Back to my home I shall not go For if I do My mother will say Did you ever see a cow with a green eyebrow Down by the Bay?* — a song that fascinated you though you never could get up the guts to ask him what the bay was, it couldn't have been the Hudson's Bay Company store in Calgary because there weren't any watermelons downtown but somehow there was an allusion in this song, a hint that your father visited some mysterious and forbidden place (you knew that just before meeting your mother he'd spent six months in South Africa shooting at Boers, which for the longest time you thought meant wild pigs) and the womenfolk asked sarcastic questions about it but he kept going anyway and each time he went he saw something different and it was always green. *Did you ever see a bear in green underwear Down by the Bay?*

17

Your mother taught you to wash your hands six times a day, say grace before meals, butter your bread economically by skip-skip-skipping across the surface of the slice with the precious yellow substance on the point of your knife, eschew fiddling with your cock, chew your food thoroughly and with your mouth closed (ideally she said each mouthful should be masticated thirty times), brush your teeth with salt and be nice to your little sister. Every night for what seemed like years she read aloud to you from *Pilgrim's Progress*, a book in which nothing was beautiful but everything was edifying, in which characters with names like Christian, Worldy-Wiseman, Obstinate and Pliable fell into the Slough of Despond or passed through the Village of Morality, in which every allegory was transparent and every move a fatal step towards heaven or hell. The precepts she glued onto your brain — A job worth doing is worth doing well, Never put off till tomorrow what can be done today, If at first you don't succeed try try again, Where there's a will there's a way — adhered to you, more than you adhered to them, for the rest of your life.

Your father taught you to finish what was on your plate and you dreaded mealtimes in advance because there was a better than even chance that your plate would contain one of those concoctions whose starchy lumpiness disgusted you, the most frequent being oatmeal porridge and potatoes — Wot yer mean, yer don't like p'taters? he would ask, his hand punctuating the question with a blow to the side of your head which would cause your ears to ring until you fell asleep that night — My old man had to leave his farm in Ireland 'cos there was no p'taters left to eat, now we got all the p'taters we want and no son of mine is going to turn up his nose at wot he's lucky enough to see on his plate! One evening he gave you the choice between eating the mound of mashed potatoes heaped in front of you and having your face rubbed in it and you chose the latter, and he got up and shoved your head down onto your plate and held it there until you had to fight for breath and when at last you came up gasping you looked so funny with your dark eyes shining out of a mask of lumpy bumpy wet white mush that Elizabeth giggled and your mother smirked in spite of herself. Occasionally Mildred would make rice pudding for dessert or, worse, tapioca or, worst of all, bread pudding with old crusts gone from dry to soggy by soaking in milk and cooked up with sugar, and your stomach would heave and your eyes would sting as you stared at them in hatred, sitting there alone at the table after everyone else had been excused.

Effusiveness was discouraged but kisses good-night were mandatory and their omission punished.

You were dragged off to church every Sunday morning and requested not to fidget on the wooden bench that pressed meanly into your skinny little ass for what seemed like hours at a time, hemmed in by your mother on one side and your sister on the other, the endless sermon boring boring boring into your forehead from up front. Oh, those sermons, Paddon! Those benevolent male voices that went up at the beginning of the sentence — I want to tell you a little story — then extended flat forever and ever as far as the ear could hear. You know, they would say, and the word *know* would go up and you would know you were in for it — You know, maybe if you'd told people a while ago, just stick a little piece of paper on an envelope and it'll go round the world, they would have thought you were crazy. But there was a vision there. And you'd be surprised what you can accomplish if you have a vision. Oh the mortal insipidity of those mealy-mouthed ministers. And your mother would nod her head in approval and admiration of their eloquence and you would want to smash yours into the pew in front of you to simply keep awake.

First Anton Methodist was a stark spare structure filled with strictures and scriptures, the idea of pointing up to heaven incorporated into its roof and rafters — not a lovely lofty movement upwards, floating through arches and vaults and pillars and flying buttresses and gothic gargoyles, but an order — a finger sternly pointing to the sky: keep your eyes on heaven! stay on the straight and narrow! keep to the point! And the points of your ass would twinge and the pain would go creeping up your backbone and dig into your shoulder-blades as the minister went on and on until at last the shrill small organ would pipe up and the closing hymn would go rolling across the plains like tumbleweed, prickly and full of emptiness. *Holy, Holy, Holy! though the darkness hide Thee Though the eye of sinful man Thy glory may not see Only Thou art holy, there is none beside Thee Perfect in power, in love, and purity.* It was then, was it then, that the seeds of your work on time were first planted, a Jack-and-the-beanstalk work that would sprout and branch and stretch up and up and finally lose itself in the clouds but you knew there were giants up there in those clouds, didn't you Paddon?

———•———

Finally you broke free of your mother's steely embrace, leaving Calgary and bolting north to Edmonton where a university had been founded ten years earlier. Those first years living away from home, in circumstances that misleadingly resembled your idea of freedom, were nothing less than euphoric. The winters were unremitting up north — no Chinooks whooshing down from the mountains to kiss the January snow to death — but your brain-fires, endlessly stoked by readings in history and philosophy, radiated warmth to the tips of your very being. Only many years later did it occur to you that these disciplines had been naïvely chosen because they appeared certain to lead you away from the murderous monotony of church services. You expected your readings to act as powerful and definitive antidotes to the poison of Eternal Truth that had been pumped into your veins since the day you were born. The theoretical paradoxes of history delighted you, for example that effects could always be traced back to their causes but that nothing could ever be predicted with certainty; you were especially relieved by the *successiveness* of history because it gave you a handle, as it were, on a reality which the specious shine of Christianity had made as impossible to grasp as your own hand in the mirror.

I think that once you had grimly endured the mandatory ridicule of freshman initiation week, during which you walked around with a V-shaped figure shaved on the back of your head, your pants rolled up and green pennants fluttering at your shoulders, you probably avoided taking part in the whole whoopla of being a student such as joining fraternities, debate clubs and football teams or flirting and boasting about panty raids in the girls' dorms. I see you alone — neither outcast nor downcast but alone, withdrawn, preferring the silent company of great dead men to the raucous one of your puerile peers. Occasionally you would join the latter for a game of poker or gin rummy, but only to avoid the additional wasted time it would have meant if excessive seriousness had designated you as their scapegoat. Your evenings were spent for the most part in the library or in your room but preferably the library because it was more generously heated, getting acquainted with Aristotle and Augustine, thrilling to their paradoxes, the abysses they pointed out to you then helped you leap across. *Before He made heaven and earth* you once read at two in the morning with your feet on the radiator *God made nothing. For if He did make anything, could it have been anything but a creature of His own creation?* This sort of paradox delighted you no end: with your mind in Augustine's you walked along paths that were often narrow but never straight and whose wild dizzying beauty was just the opposite of the vapid heavenly kingdom you had been taught to yearn for — *There we shall be with Seraphims and Cherubims*, as *Pilgrim's Progress* had told you, *creatures that will dazzle your eyes to look on them . . . every one walking in the sight of God and standing in His presence with acceptance for ever* — it had appalled you, this perspective of a world of fat little angels and stultifying virtue in which everyone stood around wearing haloes and playing lyres and admiring God on His throne *as He was in the beginning is now and ever shall be, world without end Amen.*

You discovered that time was the key to the problem of heaven while you were still an undergraduate because of a passage in Saint Augustine that had made you laugh out loud — *Although You are before time* said Augustine, addressing God, *it is not in time that You are before it. If this were so, You would not be before all time.* Or again, concerning God's inaugural decree Let there be light — *Whatever You might have used to produce the voice by which the decree was uttered, it would not have existed at all unless it had been made by You. But to create a material thing which could be used to give voice to the decree, what Word did You speak?*

You tuned your senses keenly keenly Paddon to receive this theme whenever its enigmatic melody rang forth in your readings — What sort of phenomenon was time? Was it concrete or abstract? Real or imaginary? Universal or cultural or individual? You were capable of waltzing with these questions until the break of dawn, which in the winter months was pretty near mid-morning.

But oh the lack of companionship for your lofty love. Oh the hopelessly taxidermic manner in which you were expected to stuff your precious quivering living private thoughts so as to present them motionless and dead in the form of a mid-term paper with an outline. Oh the humiliation of being required to produce twenty-five typewritten pages no more no less on one and only one facet of Aristotle's *Metaphysics*, and getting your paper back covered with nit-picking remarks in red ink and never being able to talk it over with anyone. Oh the disconcerting speed with which thinkers became statues and were hoisted onto pedestals and covered with dust. Oh the enraging peremptory blandness of your professors, standing at their lecterns like priests with their grey hair and glasses, suits and ties, reading ninety-minute lectures with scarcely a glance at the class, then packing up their briefcases and retiring to their diploma-lined offices. Whereas you, Paddon, longed to be talking things over with Descartes himself at his home in Leiden, sitting next to the fireplace and sucking on a pipe and listening to his arguments and countering them with your own until the crackling flames were glowing embers and winter dawn came sifting through the shutters . . . Or standing around the Athens gymnasium chewing the rag with Socrates . . . Or joining Goethe at Weimar for a week in the summer . . . If worst came to worst you would have settled for an evening at Nohant with George Sand and Flaubert! People caring about ideas — that was what you wanted more than anything. Not a heaven in which to sit in starry-eyed bliss. Not an embossed certificate with which to prove you had passed your predoctoral exams.

In 1922 you produced what you thought was a stunning senior paper, suggesting that Augustine's encyclopaedic knowledge and mental acuity could have been put to better use had he not squandered so much energy banging his head against that inexistent wall known as God. All the contradictions and inconsistencies the philosopher had brought to light, you argued, looping them around himself like ropes then pulling them tight and tying them into knots so as to marvel at his own paralysis, would have miraculously dissipated if he had only abandoned the premise of God's existence. *If I find You beyond my memory,* said the implacable convert, *it means that I have no memory of You. How, then, am I to find You, if I have no memory of You?* But, you the passionate atheist pursued, if You do not exist then I have only my memory, and is that not wondrous and holy enough? So wondrous and holy indeed that it is capable of inventing You? Too brash, scrawled your professor on the back of the last page, gleefully awarding you a *C.* One cannot radically transform the terms of the author's discussion and then expect to receive a passing mark for one's comprehension of the author. Be careful not to let your brilliance run away with you.

I prefer it run away with me than without me, you muttered

as you left the philosophy building, the nape of your neck aflame.

Some nights after reading for six hours straight you would stand in front of the tiny shaving-mirror that hung from a nail above the kitchen sink and stare at yourself and marvel that this form, this smooth round ball of a head with its placid forehead and motionless hair and steady eyes, should contain such unbelievable activity. That beneath the protective encasing of skin and bone were folds of oily-slick whitish matter the consistency of marrow, pulsing with involuntary electric signals by virtue of which all the information you had just absorbed had already been not only recorded but organized, categorized and connected in countless ways to pre-existing information, then stored so as to be unobtrusive yet instantly retrievable at the least command from your will — you would stare at yourself, Paddon, intensely moved at the thought of this thrumming throbbing machine, and how young you were, and how certain it was that you would go on to use its invisible impalpable power to accomplish something great, make some absolutely colossal discovery. By the time you began graduate school — moving out of the campus dorm and renting a small flat in a house on 110th Street — your body had come to seem superfluous, beside the point, a source more of annoyance than pleasure, infringing on your consciousness and forcing you back to the surface just when you wanted most avidly to be plunged in thought.

Your diet was exactly as meagre and repetitive as your love-making. Twice a day you ate canned food, once a week you went downtown and frequented the sad tired leathery bodies of Indian whores, spending your Saturday nights in the reek of stale home

brew and cheap tobacco and sleazy hallways, then walking away
Sunday mornings shivering with disgust, clutching your thin coat
to your throat with one hand and feeling your trousers whip at
your legs as you paced the garbage-dancing windswept empty side-
walks of the city, your stomach cringing with hunger and shame,
your penis curled up in your crotch like a fox in its lair after an
unsuccessful raid of the chicken coop. There was ejaculation in
these contacts but never pleasure, never even real relief, you
wished you could fuck these women and have done with it, fuck
them once and for all, fuck them and never need to fuck anyone
again, and sometimes you would vomit and consider how your
vomit on the sidewalk was evocative of a verbal expostulation, the
splotch in the centre surrounded by exclamation marks — Corn! it
seemed to be saying, or Beans with tomato sauce! Everything you
had eaten, everything you thought you had put away, was now
back and jeering silently at you — Look! your vomit said. You can
do nothing once and for all, not even eat. You would resolve to go
back to Augustine and never take your mind off him again, convinced that despite your atheism you understood and shared his
aspiration to *something that was not material beauty, or beauty of a
temporal order . . . not heaven or earth or any kind of bodily thing*, yet
the following Saturday night your loneliness would be so acute
there was nothing for it but to leave your room and walk until you
were so cold you had to enter one of those camouflaged saloons
and order a revolting mixture of rye, red ink and tobacco juice at
fifty cents a glass, setting into motion the inexorable sequence of
events that would lead you through the opening of your wallet and
your fly to the fumbling and the sprawling and the desperate
sweaty panting on the women's bodies and the humiliation of their

stroking and joking and cajoling and lapping and lipping you to a miserable spasm of self-hate, all the way to the exclamatory splash of vomit on the sidewalk the next morning. And in the midst of your Sunday shivering and disgust you knew that Elizabeth and your mother were busy getting ready for church, pulling on their wool stockings and their warmest darkest dresses, adjusting their hats in the mirror then trundling down the sidewalk arm in arm — the church bells were ringing and sometimes you thought you could hear those bells the way your father must have done, a fury of clanging jangling angry pots and pans that drove men to clap their hands over their ears as the women resolutely departed to pray for their souls. This would make you sob, but then on Monday classes would begin again and your dreams would soar like birds.

You had lit upon what you considered a brilliant topic for your doctoral dissertation: the history of time — an analysis of human conceptions and descriptions of time over the centuries — and would lie awake for hours at night overflowing with sentences and chapter headings. To your vexation but not to your surprise, the professors displayed no particular enthusiasm for this project. They frowned and voiced the opinion that it was far too broad, too ambitious and all-encompassing. You gritted your teeth and told yourself they would no doubt have said the same to Plato or Descartes. Imagine young René walking into the University of Alberta and announcing: I'd like to write a thesis on how to prove the existence of God. Or Plato: I'd like to write a thesis on the perfect city-state. The withering glances they would have received! The condescending speeches they would have had to sit through!

Surely you realize, young man, that time is one of the most copiously dealt with subjects in the history of philosophy. Merely to familiarize yourself with the existing literature on the subject would take you ten years at the very least. You were in your thesis advisor's living room, he had invited you to his home for a fuller discussion of the problem but unfortunately your throat had been parched upon arrival as it was the end of June and Edmonton's sun was pitiless and pounding so you had gulped down three glasses of lemonade and now all you could think of was your bladder, not the history of time but how soon you would be able to relieve yourself, and the professor's wife was intently listening to her husband's peroration and nodding as though this were a very serious matter indeed and you were certain that if you asked to use the bathroom she would turn to you with a stony stare and say, We don't have one. We don't do that sort of thing. You left an hour later, cowed and defeated, having been so obsessed with controlling your lower parts that you had found it impossible to defend your higher ones and done nothing but grin inanely and promise to think it over during the summer.

Then, in rapid succession, two deadly ju-jitsu blows were dealt to the neck of your dreams: your father died and you became a father.

———◦———

What I see next dates from several years later when you were already teaching high school in Calgary — the order in which your life reveals itself to me is anything but chronological, yes I can only discover you, construct you by flashes, and what I have just realized is that you must have felt as trapped by repetition between the desks of your classroom as you had between the pews of Anton Methodist.

You got up there and taught and then you got up there and taught again and then you taught again, you said the same words the students took the same notes you passed out the same exams they made the same mistakes you made the same corrections, you looked out the same window and sometimes the ground was white and sometimes it was brown and sometimes it was green and you wiped off the same blackboard and you made the same jokes with your colleagues during coffee-break and you knew the number of the year was changing as was the number of years you had been living as was the number of years you had been teaching as were the names of the students and you also knew that the students who had sat before you in the early years had grown and changed their hairstyles and clothing styles several times and gained or lost weight and married and started having children and affairs and pretty soon their children would be sitting in front of you scratching their heads with their pencils and picking their noses and eating their snot while you, the reason you were here, the point of your walking this earth would still be left a blank. And when you tried to coax your mind back onto the dizzying paths it had followed in graduate school, you could not quite remember what it was you had wanted to say, could not even quite feel the shape of the questions that had come to you in the night and made love to your mind during the magic years, before your father died and you came back south and got stuck in the mire of material necessity.

You haul sixteen tons, and what do you get? Another day older and deeper in debt . . . The real floundering began with the birth of Ruthie because you had to move and that meant taking a bigger mortgage and you realized that well yes never maybe never at all maybe not next year or the year after that but just never? And then a great confusion arose and took you in its arms, enfolding you crushing you to it mussing your hair rocking you violently scrambling your brains, so that it was all you could do to go through the motions of father husband teacher husband father teacher day after day. You would pick up the pointer and point to some essential date and suddenly you would see yourself from the outside, standing there at the blackboard arms akimbo like a puppet, and it would take a gigantic effort to wrench yourself back to the topic at hand and make it safely to the end of the hour by which time you would be thoroughly tense and your head would be throbbing and the recess bell would jolt you to and from your senses and five minutes later you would have to start all over again with another class, to say nothing of what was awaiting you at home.

So early in '32 when Karen discovered she was pregnant once again you looked at her and said Well this one's gonna have to count on God, and she said What do you mean, and you said I can't go on like this, putting food on the table while I'm dying of mental starvation, and she said But what on earth is the matter, Paddon? You have a job full of words and ideas, you get paid for thinking and teaching others to think, and you said It's killing me, can't you see that? I'm getting old, I'm already going grey, and Karen said Don't be silly, Paddon, look how lucky we are just to have a roof over our heads when so many other families these days — and you interrupted her, shouting by this time,

Don't tell me I'm lucky when I tell you I'm miserable! Karen! And as usual when you shouted she sat down suddenly, folded her hands in her lap and stared at them until two fat tears welled up in her eyes letting you know you were wounding her and this was not the man to whom she had committed herself body and soul so you lowered your voice. Karen, you said, look at it this way — I'm almost as old as Jesus was when He died, and she nodded so you went on, Think of everything Jesus had done by the time he was thirty-three, think of all the sermons all the miracles all the prayers, and Karen said very softly I don't know what you're getting at, Paddon, this is certainly the first time you've compared yourself to Jesus Christ, and you said What I'm getting at is, did Jesus ever hold down a full-time job? and she said Don't be ridiculous, and you said Or did He say, Consider the lilies of the field, they reap not neither do they sow, and Karen said Maybe you're trying to be funny but there are thousands of people in this city right this minute who reap not neither do they sow and they don't look like lilies of the field to me. And you said Just for one year, and she said Just what, and you said Just give me one year, just to see if I'm capable of something, and she said Paddon, what are you talking about? and you raised your voice again and said I'm talking about one year without setting foot in that fucking high school that's what I'm talking about, and she said Don't swear at me, I can't believe you're serious I just told you I'm going to have another baby and you're telling me you plan to stop earning money? Karen never raised her voice but she was weeping in earnest now because she knew that was exactly what you were going to do.

You continued teaching through June, watching her stomach

swell like a reproach, a threat, an angry insect bite. The principal's face when you appeared in his office to formulate your request was a study in incredulity — Sabbaticals do not exist for high school teachers, Mr. Sterling, he said. Even God needed a rest after six days of creation, you replied, wondering where all these Biblical analogies were coming from all of a sudden. Listen, Mr. Sterling, this is no time for banter, I can give you a year off but paying you even half your salary is out of the question with the economy in its present state. Think it over and let me know.

So the final cheque arrived at the end of August and was gobbled up a few days later by the maternity hospital Karen had insisted on having this time, which was understandable, and you named the new baby John — isn't that strange, I've just this second realized my uncle Johnny was named after your dead father — and then hell set in.

No, Karen did not nag and complain, she came home with the baby and swallowed her protestations and set about proving to you she was the most perfect wife in the history of the human race. You could almost hear her repeating *For better and for worse* under her breath as she moved softly around the kitchen while you tried to think in the next room which was your bedroom and also the baby's, but in a corner of which you had built yourself a desk out of orange crates covered with an old plaid bedspread. Karen's moving around the kitchen disturbed you, drew your attention by its very softness, its holier-than-thou ostentatiousness, its self-satisfied compliance with Christ's admonition to *return kind for evil.* Look, said the careful pad-padding of her slippered feet on the linoleum, you rant and rave while I do everything in my power to make you happy. Think of what I go through with my friends, how brave I have to be to stand up for you and defend you and justify what seems to them a piece of madness. These words resounded loudly in the silence. The alarm clock ticked behind you like a supervisor tapping his foot. You stuffed it beneath the pillow, noticing in spite of yourself that the pillowcase was threadbare, and rushed back over to your desk.

The door was closed when Frankie left for school at eight-thirty and you knew that Karen would respectfully refrain from opening it until twelve o'clock when she called you to partake of a lunch that was purposely made not too scant and unappetizing so you would see she was doing her best not to rub your nose in the family's poverty. The door was closed but you found yourself straining to hear everything that went on on the other side: Karen's softness, her shushing of little Ruthie playing with dolls made of potatoes and socks, her endless patient rocking of the baby when it cried . . .

And Johnny cried. Not the lusty gusty yelling bellows Frankie had let loose in the first months of his life but a constant whimpering, an endless dribble of complaint that seemed expressly designed to rub your nerves raw, undermining your concentration second by second and minute by minute until you wanted to barricade the door against that minuscule misery, pile up the beds and chairs and chests of drawers, put every piece of furniture in the world between you and your baby son's maddening mewling and your wife's conspicuous consideration.

Again and again you tried to empty your brain of external impressions, take a deep breath and tell yourself that now was the time to begin . . . But the mere idea that the following year you might have nothing to show for all this time to yourself and that Karen would be able to look at you and triumphantly not be angry, generously not be disappointed, charitably continue to love you no matter whether you had succeeded or failed — the mere idea of this deadly benevolence turned your mind to a sheet of ice.

Some days you forced yourself to write — anything was better than this flagrant fantastical paralysis — and tore up the pages as soon as they were filled and knew that Karen, just to emphasize how totally she respected your privacy, would empty the wastebasket in the evening without so much as glancing at the pitiful efforts at thinking they contained.

Other days you tried to convince yourself it was only natural that your brain should have gotten rusty after years of misuse and disuse, and it would need to be primed and oiled before you could expect it to run smoothly again. So you would stand by your board-and-brick bookcase and flip as casually as you could through the books that had elated your youth. There was Mill, there was Ruskin, there was the insurmountable Goethe — ah yes, books your father had made fun of. And you would get to thinking about your father and wondering if in fact he hadn't been embarrassed, since he himself was just barely able to read and write, and you would start feeling sorry for him and wishing you could talk to him again, and the page in front of you would go fuzzy and you would have to stamp your foot to bring it back into focus and swerve your mind violently around to its subtle argumentation.

All of this was utterly exhausting, so that when you emerged from the bedroom upon hearing Frankie bang the door at four-thirty you had to conceal your relief from Karen's anxiously sympathetic eye, and were glad to be able to drop into the armchair with the stuffing spilling out of it in three places and shake open *The Calgary Herald* and lose yourself in other people's bad news.

Ruthie was so overjoyed to see you Paddon, it made you feel ashamed. She would come over and perch shyly on the edge of your armchair and talk to you with her finger in her mouth until finally you would put away the paper and start bouncing her on your lap — *This is the way the lady rides Nimble nimble, nimble nimble This is the way the gentleman rides A gallop a trot, a gallop a trot This is the way the farmer rides Jiggety-jog, jiggety-jog* — but other times, oh Paddon other times instead of bouncing her up and down on your lap you would turn her over your knee and whack and paddle until your arm was sore. Why did you do that what on earth had Ruthie done had she playfully come up behind the newspaper and snatched it out of your hands without warning, or had she covered your eyes to play Guess Who and clumsily knocked over the reading-lamp, breaking the bulb and lightbulbs cost three cents apiece, or had she squealed so loudly with the joy of being bounced on your lap that she woke the baby who just a few minutes before had drifted off to sleep at last . . . Why did you do it Paddon why did you need to make her buttocks burn and her rosy cheeks glisten with tears and her trusting eyes cloud up with fear, your little girl who loved you all around the world and up to the sky? And then you would be mortified and try to pretend nothing had happened and jump up out of your chair and suggest a game of hide-and-seek with Frankie and feel relief flood into your chest as Ruthie's face brightened and her eyes darted about in search of the ideal impregnable place to hide.

Then Karen would call you all to supper and surreptitiously murmur grace beneath her breath and the day would be nearly done and you would not approach your wife's body during the night, telling yourself it was because she needed her sleep, being up so often with the baby whose colicky cry drilled holes into the darkness of your room . . .

Another dream, or shreds of sentences referring to another dream, probably dates from about this time:

> . . . *hearing the real or imagined cry of a child — my inner pictures suddenly freezing into a hideous array of bulbous bodies and grotesque postures — all mothers and children — mouths askew like wryly smirking cunts — seams of features where no features should have been — click, click — the picture changing as in a slideshow — babies, bodies, stubby nubby chins and knees and cheeks and buttocks — click, click — the show of mock concern, mother instinct — click, click — the stitched cunt, the stitched mouth, all these quasi-people sprawled in a stinking farmyard and liking it — click, click — as if the smooth horrifying stumps of arms and legs were their noble heads and shoulders — click, click — the child's cry, the mother's worried mouth, her knitted brow — click, click — the knitting-needles had sewn all the mutilated members into one inseparable mass . . .*

Back to the farmyard, was that it? Meanwhile back at the ranch? Back in Anton between your mother's knitting-needles and the stench of horse manure?

Having resolved to take notes, you furiously copied passages from books and quotations from the newspaper, jotting down your own ideas which were now mere memories of the ideas you had had ten years before and sounded like platitudes even before they had been laid flat on the page. The weeks went by and you gradually began putting sheaves of paper into folders and piles of folders under books, now it looked as if you were working but after all, anything and everything could be said to be related to the subject of time and you had no idea how far each nook and cranny of this cavernous subject should be explored. You went downtown to the public library and stood among its stacks and selected one book after another, bringing home a dozen thick tomes only to wonder with a sinking feeling what good it would do anyone to see your own book, one day, on the shelf among the others. You dropped the borrowed books through the return slot, went home and glared in revulsion at the mess on your desk.

The following week, resolving to go about things differently, you pushed aside the heaps of other people's words, took a fresh sheet of paper and started concocting an outline. Now, you asked yourself in an inner voice whose forced geniality could not quite fool your inner ears, should I approach the subject chronologically, geographically or from a purely philosophical point of view? Is there not some elegant way to combine all of these approaches? Tentative chapter titles began to appear, neatly aligned at first then branching out into headings and subheadings with arrows and question marks pushing you onto the back of the page, then asterisks referring you to page 1A, then 1B so that by the end of the week there were fifteen pages of confusion and frustration scattered across your desktop. That evening it was Frankie's turn to get walloped.

The week after that, making a fresh start on Monday as one

of your mother's precepts had suggested, you decided to relax and follow the natural flow of your thoughts and trust them to take on coherent shapes and structures, so you began writing on page one but by the time you reached page five on Friday there were sixty-odd footnotes, several of which were threatening to become chapters in themselves.

No relief was afforded you by sleep, for in your sleep you continued to write and although the work itself sometimes went more smoothly it invariably disappeared the minute your back was turned. You would have the impression of having written one solid chapter, forty or fifty pages of intense brilliant argumentation, but upon reopening the folder you would find nothing but a couple of nearly empty sheets. However much you wrote, you had always written nothing. Reams of typewritten material turned out to be, rather than the finished product, simply additional notes. Frantically you would search your study for the real thing, the manuscript which after endless excruciating struggle you had finally managed to bring to fruition, to completion, moving piles of books around, lifting ashtrays, peering under calendars — ah, here it was, but no that wasn't it, it was nowhere to be found, it had never existed, and when you woke up that would be the truth — it did not exist, at least not yet, not today, no more today than yesterday — and you would try to calm your rising panic, Paddon, try to view the whole thing from a distance, approach it methodically and accept the slowness of its progress, like the little train bravely inching its way up the hill and saying to itself I think I can I think I can I think I can, only now you had really begun to fear that you could not.

That was what it was like for the first few months, and then it got worse. Because those months were behind you and there were only as many left ahead of you before teaching would reclaim your soul. You felt the beginning and the end of this precious year closing in on you like two solid brick walls and could only cower in the present, waiting to be crushed.

———————— • ◦ • ————————

I'm filled with trepidation about this process, Paddon, this gradual pulling of your existence from the void like coloured scarves from the hat of a magician. The more I learn, the more I realize I don't know. Every answer raises a dozen new questions. Last night I managed to decipher another fragment of your manuscript, and it took my breath away.

> *Sometimes too (but this must have been several years later) I'd be talking to Miranda, or rather lying in her arms and listening to her talk, and suddenly, instead of spinning gently, rhythmically, regularly from between her lips like a spider's sparkling strand, her sentences would emerge as a solid block of sound, uttered in a single, inchoate, definitive squawk. I would find myself running madly down the street, then waking up and trying to control the pounding of my heart.*

Who is Miranda?

So you would wake up wild with fear and what could you possibly reveal of your nightmares to Karen especially if Miranda was someone in whose arms you lay — oh Grandpa I'm so proud of you if it's true — and Karen would confide her worry about her husband to her friends in the neighbourhood and solicit their advice over coffee and spice-cake and pass the word in clandestine letters or hushed telephone conversations to the rest of your family, especially Elizabeth, so they could include you in their prayers . . .

Poor, sweet Paddon.

———————◆———————

None of the fear was dissolved or transformed into anything essentially different until you met Miranda. By that time Johnny was five years old and a chronic thumb-sucker and mommy-clinger, by that time failure had coursed through all the sluices of your being, God still hadn't gotten tired of grinding His heel into the Palliser Triangle, soil-drifts were ten feet high and cattle bones lay scattered like mysterious white pictograms on the bracken fields, farmers were eating gophers, city folks staggered about like automatons in their baggy clothes, the world was withering to nothingness and then one day.

And then one day, in the darkest coldest depths of a winter that seemed intent on dragging humanity into the dregs forever, what with fascist bombs exploding in Spain and the Nazis rubbing their hands together in Germany and peasants being starved to death in Russia and a loud-barking dog having its vocal chords removed in Buffalo New York, one day, a Saturday on which Karen had the flu and had asked you just this once to do the shopping, you went to the market to see what could be bought. Maybe turnips, maybe carrots, maybe potatoes or cabbage for the stomachs of your children, a pound of lard if you were very lucky. When you left the house it was thirty below and pitch-dark. You walked with your head down, turning its emptiness over and over and marvelling at it as though you had never seen it before, stopping to warm yourself in every open shop along the way, reaching the grocery store just as the sun was setting fire to the Rocky Mountains. And then.

A small crowd had already gathered round the vegetable stalls, mostly women, words and vapour pouring from their mouths as they squabbled over prices and bemoaned shortages and cursed temperatures and cluck-clucked about the King, the British Empire's beloved Edward who had committed the folly of falling in love with an American and a married one at that, you were just bracing yourself to join them when you noticed, off to one side, a woman with paint in her hair. She was part if not all Indian. Unlike the others she was not wearing a woollen hat, her hair was long and thick and rippling and matted black with flecks and speckles of bright colour at nine o'clock on a mid-December morning. She was standing there with a bemused look on her face, and as you approached the gaggle of gossipers she caught your eye and you caught hers and as you stood there holding eyes, you stopped dead in your tracks. Paddon, you were not expecting this, ever, to happen. You just loved her.

You were not strangers to one another, no, you recognized each other instantly, the only strange thing was your never having seen this woman before whereas she had always existed inside of you. How could you possibly not know each other's names? Yet you had to exchange them, get through that formality at least despite the fact that you were already inside her. The first words you pronounced were You have paint in your hair, and she burst out laughing, a laugh that mocked you and loved you and pulled you strong and close against her like a rope. Your body jerked back into existence. You stood side by side as

41

though you had been born that way and ordered your turnips and had them weighed and counted out the nickels and coppers from your change-purses with stiff red fingers, laughing inwardly all the while, and it was clear to you that you would spend the rest of the morning and then the rest of your life discovering this woman's world.

Miranda took you to the shed she lived in with her daughter Dawn who was away, she explained, spending the weekend with her father. The place was full of cats and plants, curling tendrils and tails, dirty paint cans and teacups, scattered clothes and schoolbooks, and though the temperature indoors suggested poverty as compellingly as the neighbourhood out-of-doors you must have found its disorder exhilarating by contrast with the Scandinavian spic-and-spanness of your own home. She removed her coat and your coat and you saw that she was small and full of flesh and good rippling bubbling strength, your head and blood spun to see her and the colours in her dark hair and on her hands and on her walls. Never in your life before had a woman removed your coat and she now removed your boots as well but it was not the same thing as your mother yanking off your father's boots, and she rinsed cups and poured tea for both of you because though it was warmer in the shed than out-of-doors it was still considerably less than toasty warm. As she poured the tea she kept laughing very softly and inwardly and you still had not exchanged more than a dozen words.

Then when the tea had been drunk and some human language produced — she was a painter of paintings, you learned, but also a carpenter, a doer of things with her hands such as you were not and had never dreamed of being, she had insulated the shed herself and hammered down floorboards and cut windows into the ceiling and covered the walls with leaping shapes of paint — when more blocks of wood had been shoved into the stove and all the other pieces of clothing removed like so many extraneous details, Miranda tossed your entire slate of pluses and minuses out the window and threw her arms around you and took you home. She led you to her bed and a wide bed it was, two mattresses side by side covered with heavy patterned blankets, there was nowhere else to go and you had never wanted to be anywhere else ever, just this, just this warmth of the inside of her lower lip and this wetness of her sex beneath your fingers, just this tightness of her lips around your cock and this strength of her hands on your buttocks, just this musk between her breasts and these smooth brown hairless underarms, just this roundness of her belly as she straddled you, her face invisible behind the matted painted hair, just these reiterated low cries of joy and she had to learn your name didn't she to moan it over and over again like that, this was where you had always been going Paddon and now you had finally arrived.

Snow was swirling and the sky lead grey when you emerged from Miranda's shed, the morning was over and Karen was probably wondering where you were, you felt extremely close to Karen as you walked towards her with your new body, extremely tender and protective carrying the turnips, and suddenly the word for what had happened came into your mind, the word *adultery*, and you remembered the first time you had heard it, when your mother was teaching you the Ten Commandments and she got to *Thou shalt not commit adultery* and you said What's adultery? and she slapped you across the face and told you never to use that word again, then all through your childhood you had thought it must be something done only by adults amongst themselves, adultery, keeping it secret from all children, and later still you spent time wondering about *adulterate*, adding something to a mixture so it was spoiled — was this what you had now done to your marriage, made it impure by the addition of a foreign or inferior substance? No — walking home you went over all these words in your mind and they seemed so inappropriate you laughed out loud. And heard Miranda's laughter in response for she was with you as you walked, she had entered your body and you knew that you would never be alone again.

That afternoon King Edward ascended Augusta Tower where there was a powerful radio antenna and in a choked uncertain voice informed the world of his decision to renounce his reign for love of Mrs. Simpson. His voice gathered strength as the speech went on so that by the time he reached the final phrases he was fairly shouting, God bless you all! God save the King!

And God of course agreed to do just that, to take the very best care of all those bereft and weeping British subjects as their starry-eyed butterfly-stomached monarch boarded the destroyer *Fury* and departed England for a destination unknown — perhaps his cherished EP ranch near Calgary? Oh yes, God would heap countless blessings upon the British in the years immediately following that fateful Saturday of December 1936.

Later many months later as you lay in Miranda's bed reminiscing about how you had met, you said What's amazing is that there was no nonsense whatsoever, only love. Hmm? she said, stroking one of her cats who were so numerous you never even tried to learn their names because they came and went, stray cats and alley cats and the baby cats friends would have smothered if Miranda had not taken them in. The love, you went on, of mature people who have had the nonsense knocked out of them and the sense knocked into them. What's wrong with nonsense? Miranda asked. Rolling around on the floor with Dawn, isn't that nonsense? I love being silly. Hey, come and be silly with me, Paddon.

You were shaken. What's wrong with nonsense? The people you knew didn't talk that way. You mean it's okay to like nonsense? Miranda said these things to you as casually as she revealed her nakedness, and you found them just as overwhelming.

It was shortly before the war that your grandfather stopped exploding, I remember Mother telling me several years ago. He'd exploded all through our childhood and into the thirties, she said, and then it simply ceased. Quite abruptly. For ages Johnny kept up the habit of cringing in Dad's presence, she added, flinching whenever he so much as raised his hand at table to reach for the salt. I don't think Johnny has ever really forgiven him — you notice he almost never comes to family reunions — but he's a sweet boy. You and Michael always liked him better than your other uncles and aunts, didn't you, darling?

Although she is only in her early sixties, Mother finds it difficult to keep her mind focused on a single topic especially if the topic is a painful one like the explosions of the father she so worshipped — you. She generally allows her train of thought to wander off the track and drift towards softer things, more cushiony things, more upholstered and downy things than slaps across the face, belts across the buttocks, and especially those animal howls of rage that shredded her sanity like teeth year after year. Ah . . . not often, she told me — no, not that often.

But not seldom enough that we didn't need to be constantly on guard. What is clear is that this little girl learned to avert her gaze while looking straight into someone's eyes, to plug her ears while keeping her arms pinned to her sides, to run and hide in the closet without budging from the spot on which her beloved father stood before her and howled. This talent for inner subterfuge and denial, so necessary to her survival as a child and so useful when, as a rebellious teenager later on, she felt compelled to sleep with every man who took her out for a meal, has turned my mother into a rather dithering soft-hearted old woman.

Miranda was not pretty but she was beautiful because her eyes were always dancing and her hands moving and her body so very much alive. The second time you went to her shed you went with an intuition, no a powerful sense of certainty you had arrived at in the meantime, that Miranda's father was dead, as yours was, and that this was something as crucial to her as it was to you. You told her about it the minute she opened the door to let you in, and from the way she looked at you then you knew she would also be able to love you with something other than laughter.

She did not tell you about her father that day except to say that he had died of alcoholism, that slow form of suicide available to people who do not have the nerve to use the faster forms — though many Indians did have the nerve, in fact more and more of them every year were inserting rifles into their mouths or drawing knives across their wrists or hurling themselves in front of moving trains, the only method they never resorted to was hanging because the noose makes it impossible to expel one's final breath, thus trapping the soul inside the body forever and preventing it from going on to the next world, they never could forgive the whites for having inflicted that particular penalty on some of them, that horrifying state of suspension between two states of being.

She did not tell you about her father but she did tell you other tales, lying next to you in bed her body lined up with yours but her eyes staring at the ceiling, the tales she had learned as a child so very different from those of *Pilgrim's Progress*, tales of treachery and loss and abandonment, and as you listened you knew you were hearing something true and sacred, truer and more sacred than anything you had ever heard in church, and you wondered how on earth you would be able to teach another history class full of thundering silences.

She had grown up on the Gleichen reserve southeast of town, her father was pure Blackfoot, great-nephew of the great Chief Crowfoot himself, her mother the result of a Sarcee woman's rape by a white man, she did not tell you that tale yet either, this was only the second day, but she did show you the Blackfoot–English reader that had belonged to her father in 1886, just one year after the CPR line was connected up coast to coast.

I been workin' on the railroad All the livelong day I been workin' on the railroad Just to pass the time away . . . My father's people, said Miranda, moved to the reserve after more than half of them had starved to death, but they were still determined to stop the CPR surveyors. Those guys came one morning and saw every brave in the tribe ready and willing to kill them so they said Oh oh what should we do, and their bosses said Why don't we send in good old Albert Lacombe to explain things to them — you knew about Father Lacombe, Paddon, knew he had always been the idol and the model of your sister, and almost gasped for joy

47

when Miranda referred to him as that missionary bastard — That missionary bastard was busy improving us for thirty years already, he spoke our language, he had a finger on our waning pulse, he came to talk things over bringing a couple hundred pounds of tea and sugar and flour and tobacco and what do you expect, Crowfoot bowed his head again. The CPR was so grateful they gave Lacombe a lifetime pass on the steel. But the really smart thing was — Miranda's voice rose in scathing sarcasm and your heart leaped up to join it, Paddon, no one had ever talked to you like this before — they also gave Crowfoot a lifetime pass on the steel!

You saw the old chief hoisting himself warily into one of the cars, the iron horse snorting steam and belching smoke and taking off with a roar, the prairies Crowfoot had known and loved since childhood whirring by in a blur, trees melting together, shadow and sunlight flashing blindingly. For hours and days and nights, Crowfoot tore across the plains and forests, sick at heart and mind, unable to eat or sleep, all the way to Montreal. And that was the end: At that moment, said Miranda, our people were defeated forever. Crowfoot understood the whites were not going to be a few hundred and then a few hundred more. He saw the houses where they lived piled on top of each other, he saw their high stone buildings and carriages and cobbled streets, their big glass windows full of food and clothes, and he knew the fight was over. The gift had stabbed him in the back. By the time he came back West he was no longer a chief.

A while later you read Lesson XIV out loud together as though it were funny, as though it were very very funny, as though you were actors in a hilarious comedy about the Canadian Pacific

Railway, trading roles so that she read in English while you stuttered gutturally through the Algonkian: *Look! the cars are coming. Sâtsit! istsi-enakâs epoxapoyaw. They come very fast. Ixka-ekkami-poxapoyaw. They come from Winnipeg. Mikutsitartay omort-sipoxapoyaw. The cars are full of people. Matapix itortoyitsiyaw enakâsix. Let us go to the depot. Konnê-etâpoôp istsi-enakâs-api-oyis.*

And as you walked home that afternoon those sentences kept spinning in your head — Look! the cars are coming Look! the cars are coming Look! the cars are coming They come very fast They come very fast They come very fast The cars are full of people The cars are full of people The cars are full of people — they come very fast indeed, you've never seen anything come so fast in your lives and there's nothing you can do to stop them, so Go West young man — ah, that arousing fantasy of tearing away frontiers like petticoats, the indefinitely prolonged rape of virgin land by muscle and gun — Go West, and so saying we pushed forward, shoving the natives ahead of us — Go West, we told you! — until they had their backs up against the Rocky Mountains, then toppling them over and crushing them under the inexorable advance of our caterpillar treads, then telling them Hey don't worry, here's some guns for you guys too and we'll buy up every buffalo robe you can bring us, every skin of elk gazelle deer bighorn otter and beaver so go to it, whoopee, kill 'em all! You can do better than the Assiniboines and the Crees and the Shoshone and the Kootenay and the Salish so go to it, whoopee, kill 'em all! Okay now that there's no buffalo left we'll teach you how to raise cattle and grow wheat, on condition you just stay put here on the reservation. Okay now that your crops have failed and you're starving we'll feed you, but in exchange we want half of that space back, but look, you guys get the better half and that way we can put the railroad through down here. We'll just add another little trunk-line up here through your territory, but don't worry you won't feel a thing. Okay we'll give you some money in exchange for the horses killed by passing trains and the wild game spooked off into the woods and the fields burned to the ground by sparks from spinning wheels but don't you worry now everything's going to be all right, have a drink. Have a drink. Have another drink. All right, see? Hit the gutter. *Oh give me a home where the buffalo roam Where the deer and the antelope play Where seldom is heard a discouraging word And the skies are not cloudy all day* — EVERYBODY NOW! *Home, home on the range* . . . Go West young man, we sang, grinding the bones and blood of their ancestors into cement with which to build our houses, our skyscrapers, our solid grey dreams.

Strong and free, you guys. Don't you forget it. *Fortis et Liber.* Motto of the province of Alberta.

———•◦•———

You wrote, and I have no way of knowing when:

> *Miranda is dead now. Yes, now she is dead*
> *Unless, that is, I choose to think about a different now —*
> *which is always possible.*

And for me, Paddon, your *now* has also become a *then*, and like Miranda you can go on living only in my words — only here on the pages I keep mucking up with my tears and ashes. It's such a dizzying responsibility — I'm like a tightrope-walker secreting, spiderlike, the rope on which she must continue to advance. I've never written anything like this before — my usual source of inspiration is last night's AP dispatches.

Shall I manage to breathe enough life into this rapidly fading history to quicken it into story?

———— • ————

Only once she knew how ill she was did Miranda allow you to watch her paint. She would set up her easel and wheelchair beneath the skylights, turn her back to you and ask you not to talk but she herself would talk to you every now and then as she worked. My people always painted, she said, the walls of our homes always told the stories of our lives, our adventures and especially our dreams. My canvases are just little bits and pieces of a skin house, since we're not allowed to live in them anymore. She would laugh — Look! Isn't this the finest green? — and glance at you over her shoulder, pivoting slightly in the wheel-chair to catch your eye, then resume plastering the canvas with brightness, splashes and daubs of colour — now, now — and your eyes would stare as you drank it in, the way her arm moved from palette to canvas and from canvas to palette, hovering in the air — now — that burnished red there, yes — and the mustard yellow here — and now, and now, yes right now came that inimitable blue-green.

Another time she said, Dawn's just the same as my painting. How's that? you said. Well, said Miranda, I look at her, her eyes pour things out to me and I drink them in, it could just go on and on, she fills me up with colours. You know? Mmm, you said. There's a flow, that's what counts, said Miranda. It doesn't matter what direction, it's the same thing that moves my hand to paint, and the colours that come onto the canvas laugh just the same way as Dawn. And it's always full, no matter when I stop. There's no such thing as an empty place in the world. Even the sky is full, even without a single cloud or bird.

She stopped painting, turned and added with an impish grin, That's what the white man never could understand. You guys thought this land was empty! And outwardly you laughed but inwardly you admonished yourself gravely, telling yourself not to forget what she had just taught you, believing her so fervently you were certain your mind would never again be a blank, and that evening you wrote it down just to make sure, just to make sure you were sure and would not forget.

> *There is no such thing as emptiness. The picture is always complete. Even had Scarlatti contented himself with transcribing the notes played by his cat, the piece would have been there.*
> *From a single eyelash the entire person can be reconstructed.*
> *Every part contains the whole.*

The following week Miranda lost her right shoulder. Yet she picked up where she had left off about her daughter and her art: It's the same *matter*, you know what I mean? — the body that came out of me in gushes of my blood and now she's there, just her very own self with her shape of moving flesh and her own blood inside of her and her eyes wet — that's not a different thing from my paints when I mix them and the powder wets and muds and I see something coming onto the canvas and my smock gets all streaked with red and brown but there it is, it looks like it might be a boat, and the curve of the boat appears in my daughter's eye, and the colours of the dream she told me this morning keep flowing through my hands, and each separate thing is full, you see? The canvas is full even before I begin to paint and Dawn's soul was full the day she was born and what we add shouldn't make the fullness crowded or confused, it should just move the meanings around.

You sat on one of the kitchen chairs and marvelled that Miranda should be there and still be there and still be there, pivoting her wheelchair now towards you now towards the easel, smiling, closing her eyes once in a while because painting fatigued her now but even her fatigue and even her sleep were part of the same present, a present like a sun that shone continually upon you, smoothing the frown between your eyebrows and turning your heartbeat to music.

And all the while you knew Paddon — even as you sunbathed in her philosophy of the present — as of 1943 anyway you knew that Miranda's body was a mined field and that time was advancing stealthily across it, pulling the fuse on one hand grenade after another then running back to burst into screaming laughter — haha! hahahahahaha! — and point its finger at the newly paralyzed limb.

In 1943 Miranda still had the use of her arms and hands but her legs had been inert for a year already and there were patches of insensitivity on her stomach and at the small of her back. Lying in bed you would help her draw the map of her body. Here? Kissing her. Yes. And here? Yes. And here? No — there, there is nothing. Nothing? Tracing the outline of the numb island. Paddon the cartographer, the surveyor. Rubbing the flesh of her stomach as if to warm it, as if its problem were something as banal and curable as frostbite. Darling . . . you mean you can't feel this at all? I can feel it, but it doesn't concern me. She would smile. Lying on her, looking down at her, you would stare behind her smile and try to detect a hint of terror but there was none, none whatsoever, she would smile and stroke your hair and run a blunt finger down your nose, you would shudder as your sex grew hard again and close your eyes and try to drown yourself in her. Later in the street your body would feel like a bleeding gum or a mucous membrane, so open it was, so hopelessly attached to this woman's strength and to the fact of her being alive.

After a while though, after a few years, after three or four episodes of this strange illness, each more ruthless than the last, each leaving her a little clumsier, a little shakier and with a little less of herself to share with you, it was no longer possible to join your bodies.

And you returned to your manuscript, overcome with love for Miranda and dismay at what was going on. And you wanted her to understand what she was helping you to understand:

> The cat goes forward, it cannot go backwards. But we can go backwards — otherwise there was no point in giving us so intricate a brain. This is humanity — this capacity to go back and forth, discerning forms, appreciating patterns, making connections. To be present in the past and past in the present. Even, dazzlingly, to project the future.

This was what you were going to be able at last to say, Paddon. It was what Miranda had taught you, this marvel of memory, this indestructibility of the past, and just as your mind began to close in on these ideas, trembling to see them emerge so clearly at long last, approaching them ever so carefully lest they take flight before you managed to encircle them with words — just then, Miranda started to forget.

One day she began the story of Cough Child and got side-tracked into talking about the spectacular case of mumps Dawn had had as a child and then launched into a description of a Bella Coola Indian mask that looked as if it had swollen thyroid glands, so that when you gently steered the conversation back to Cough Child she broke off, hurt, as though her mind had been striving towards something beyond the mask and now you had shut that away from her forever. And you were so sorry. And so confused. Asking yourself whether indeed it was objectively preferable to talk about one thing at a time, and if so, why. Perhaps it was better just to let the talking meander like a mountain stream and appreciate the scenery it took you past? Perhaps Miranda was right again?

Yet the next time you saw her she seemed better so you asked her directly about Cough Child and she told you the story from beginning to middle to end with no digressions. She herself had been tiny when it happened but she recalled the shiver of excitement that had gone through many on the reserve and also her father's brooding resentment. Cough Child was a Stoney, an old old man who could remember all the way back to the days before reservations. One day he woke from sleep and said he'd had a strong vision, the Great Spirit had told him to spend four nights in a row on a mountaintop and daub white paint on his cheeks every time he heard a thunderclap. Then he was supposed to return to his people and heal their diseases, teach them to pray as they did in the olden days and smoke the medicine pipe. So Cough Child obeyed, he left Morley, covered himself with white paint and went up to the mountains, and when he came back down he started healing people all over the prairies.

Crees would send for him from up north and Sarcee came out from Calgary to consult him. Every time he cured someone he would sell them a feather against thunder and tell them to daub their cheeks with white paint for good measure.

Miranda's voice drifted off. You did not see the point of the story, you had expected it to be an explanation of the Indian's name. Why was he called Cough Child? you asked. She looked at you blankly. I don't know, some say Cough Child and some say Calf Child, he lived a really long time, that's for sure. When he finally died it was an accident, he was trying to defend this cow against a pack of dogs but he slipped on the ice and the cow smashed his skull. But why did your father hate him? Don't you see? Because he said if we wanted to survive we had to paint ourselves white. And you caught your breath and nodded, reaching across the table to take her hands in yours.

So that day she had all her wits about her and you felt quite adamant about her recovery.

Two weeks later she asked you whether she had ever told you the story of Cough Child.

You were stymied by the problem she was raising. If two years had elapsed, her question would not have been upsetting. But if she had forgotten about telling you the story two weeks ago, she must also have forgotten the way you had grasped her hands to assure her of your love and understanding. Whom was she talking to? Today she was talking to a man who, in her mind, had not grasped her hands across the table after listening to the story of Cough Child. What else was missing from the long and secret past the two of you had shared? Was this going to get worse? Would she forget you had been lovers? Forget the wounds inflicted on you by your father? Forget the subject of the book you so badly needed to write? These stinging questions, once stirred, swarmed like a hornet's nest and drove you to panic. Apart from Dawn, for fleeting moments, no one had been witness to your love. It existed only in your memories and if Miranda's memory faded you would be alone as you had never been before, as no human being deserved to be alone. And if Miranda died . . . for years you refused to finish this sentence, even in your head.

You dared not try to write while this was happening but the fist of anxiety squeezing your entrails seemed ironically to energize your mind, you felt brighter and more alert than you had in years, you studied the contours of every detail you could glean from newspaper and radio about the war in Europe, the new strategic airport at Namao, the Alaskan highway rolling forth from Edmonton at breathtaking speed, slicing through the very muskeg and forest and swamp your gold-hungry old man had slugged across on dogsled a mere fifty years before — you registered everything but only so as to pour it into Miranda's ears in hopes of drawing her back to the world of causes and effects. She would listen and nod; less and less often she would ask a question, absently rubbing her dead right hand with her living left.

One day you brought your daughter Ruthie who was not yet my mother to meet Miranda, Ruthie was fifteen at the time and had dreams of becoming an artist, you had told her — though it was reckless of you, you could not help blurting out such things sometimes — that you had a friend who painted and she had nagged at you until you promised to take her to the shed, and walking there from school during lunch-hour you had asked her to keep this outing a secret between the two of you, and she had shrugged maturely as though this went without saying and your heart had chimed with gratitude, at last a bridge was going to be thrown between your two worlds.

Miranda was sitting in her wheelchair when you arrived, smoking a pipe. Dawn was there too which surprised you but then you almost never came at this time of day, she was chewing on a balogna sandwich and when she caught sight of your daughter she scowled darkly, clearly she had no intention of exchanging social niceties with this blonde-braided bobby-socked white girl on pretext that their parents were shacking up together. What can Ruthie have felt? I think my mother Ruthie took in, swallowed and digested the entire situation in a single instant and understood it to be so full there was no room for shock or any other emotion of her own; she saw that what was happening had been happening for a long time and that Dawn had always known about it and could tell that she had not and was curious to see if she would blush or blunder, so she simply gulped and got a hold of herself and bravely unfazedly stuck out her hand to Miranda. Miranda gave her a smile, gesturing with the pipe to her right hand lying inert in her lap, so Ruthie bent over and planted a kiss on her forehead. Dawn burped. Ruthie hello, said Miranda, I think I heard more about you than you heard about me — Ruthie glanced at you and said nothing — but to catch up all you got to do is look around.

While Ruthie made a slow tour of the room, gazing intently at the paintings to prove they were her only reason for being there, carefully skirting the table at which Dawn sat hunched and munching, you stood in strained silence behind Miranda's wheelchair with your hands on her shoulders, one of which she could feel and the other of which she could not, you squeezed them both and her hand went up to the left. The atmosphere was impossibly electric so within a few minutes Dawn, still glowering, wiped her mouth with her hand, shoved her chair back, grabbed her satchel and banged out the door. Miranda shrugged her shoulders more or less symmetrically. You relaxed a notch.

As she completed her second circling of the room, politely oblivious to the tension she knew her presence had created, Ruthie announced to your astonishment — this was the first you had heard of it — I want to study art in Toronto when I get out of school. Yes, said Miranda immediately, as though picking up the thread of a familiar conversation. Go far away, always an artist must go far away. Sometimes inside, sometimes outside. I myself only got as far as Calgary — she laughed but not self-deprecatingly — because of my family. But you, you can do anything you want. And I sure hope you do. What does she mean? you wondered. Doesn't Ruthie have a family?

She is beautiful, beautiful on the edge of life, Paddon, Miranda said to you later, smiling up at you as you came back to her wheelchair after seeing your daughter out the door. Then she looked down and shielded her eyes with her left hand and spoke in a low fast voice, Paddon listen to me I'm on the edge of life too and you got to listen. I can't paint much longer because there's too much light and I know I'm starting to forget because my head is filling up with light too. So I want to tell you something right now Paddon before I forget it, and just listen and don't talk, all right? I want to tell you how things should be when I die. Miranda, you said, hating the high-pitched phoney tone of your own voice, the doctors haven't said anything about dying, they haven't even made a diagnosis yet, but she interrupted you saying Paddon, I told you to shut up, now will you just shut up and listen? I know I'm gonna die so don't be stupid and not listen to me now 'cause you'll be sorry later. You're gonna die too and I hope you know that. This is just one way of dying, maybe a little faster than your way but you know, I'm going on forty, my mom died before she got that far, I'm just lucky I didn't die when I was a baby like my brothers and sisters 'cause I wouldn't have got to meet you and that would have been a damn shame. Hey, Paddon, that's what I wanted to tell you — I'm happy. We had a lot of years already and boy you made me happy — lots of good laughing you brought me, so many times, even when I wasn't making fun of you! And don't you dare think I'm dying because we done something bad. That's nothing but Christian guilt crap. I'm not going with my head hanging down on my chest and I'll be really mad if you can't behold yourself and walk with your head up too. You hear me?

You nodded but could not speak and Miranda thought you were overcome and she was right, but it was because she had said behold yourself instead of behave yourself. This was not the first time you had noticed a tiny slippage in her speech, some-times it was a hestitation sometimes a repetition and sometimes an inappropriate choice of words but always it upset you, like the flickering of a lightbulb which meant that sooner or later, inevitably, a fuse would blow.

Both the content and the form of Christian church services are annihilations of time: the content because it describes truth as revealed and creation as instantaneous, the form because of its absolute predictability.

You felt as threatened by one as by the other, drowning in the infinity of God's wisdom and the eternity of His love, battered over the head by the relentless monotony of hymns and sermons and Sunday school.

Your father did not go to church because he almost invariably spent his Sunday mornings nursing the consequences of his Saturday nights, he was rarely even dressed when Mildred came home with her conscience as spanking clean as her Sunday shoes, having prayed for him so thoroughly she now had the right to needle and berate him for the remainder of the week. Elizabeth's faith was far more fervent than her mother's; by the time she was five there was always a quote from the Bible or the hymn-book on her lips and when her father gave her a thrashing she would lie there flat on his lap and sing out bravely *I will not be afraid I will not be afraid, I shall go onward, and ever onward And not be afraid* — it took all the fun out of it for him. You little Paddon were the only one in the house in front of whom John Sterling could behave with what he considered manliness — and you knew it. If you allowed yourself to be cornered in the bedroom your father's blows could rain on you silently for interminable minutes without the least clap of vocal thunder to arouse the suspicion of the females cluck-ing and cooking in the kitchen.

Why did he hurt you so badly?

Sometimes it was to teach you a lesson. There was the time you were three or four years old and hanging around the woodshed watching him saw firewood, loving the silent golden rain of sawdust onto snow, and noticed an axe lying on the woodpile and went over to lick the frost from it and got your tongue stuck, and he led you by the ear all the way to the kitchen with the axe hanging off your tongue and your eyes popping out from the pain and poured a huge pitcherful of cold water over your head, laughing uproariously as the axe came away taking the tender pink skin of your tongue with it and the water ran down your back and into your underpants.

Or there was the frozen ears day. You started school in the winter of '06 and it was the worst winter in human memory in human history in human possibility. You were luckier than most ranch kids because the elementary school in Anton was a mere forty-five-minute walk from your house rather than a ninety-minute ride on horseback, but a lot of pain can happen in forty-five minutes. You would set foot out of doors when it was still pitch-dark and of course there was nothing to be afraid of in a just-barely-six-year-old boy walking three miles along an icy slippery cruddy rutted road in the dark except that your eyeballs seized up in shock the instant they encountered the cold and your brow froze into frightened furrows and your fingers no longer knew whether they were curled up to steal the warmth of your palms or stretched out straight in the woollen fingers of your gloves. By the time you got to school your thighs were stiff and wooden, your feet had turned into blocks of rock and even your buttocks ached. The coal stove hunched in the middle of the one-room schoolhouse was either konked out, in which case you kept your coats and scarves on during classes and counted on the accumulated body heat of fifty children to get you through the day, or else pouring smoke down your throats and noses, and even on the rare days it was working properly the children who sat near it cooked and those on the periphery shivered uncontrollably. Then one day — tussle in the cloakroom — your toque was grabbed from you and teasingly tossed in the air — you were pig-in-the-middle, desperate to get it back — the teacher materialized — what was the name of that strict red-haired red-tempered Scottish lady? — saw that the toque had scratched white streaks on the soot-coated ceiling — and, asking no questions, confiscated it.

Catastrophe. Walking home without a toque. Dark pitch-dark at four in the afternoon. Wind whipping screaming warning you of what was going to happen when you got home. Turning up your collar pulling up your scarf covering your ears with your hands and rubbing them with your gloves but they disappear just the same, dissolve into nothingness, the blood circles too thinly through their narrow rims and ripples and cannot keep on flowing under the brutal assaults of such a wind, it slows and stops. Your father sees you coming over the rise without your toque on and is waiting for you at the gate. He asks no questions either, except rhetorical ones such as Why d'yer think yer mother knits 'erself blind? that fade in and out of your hearing as his blows fall directly onto your naked culpable frozen white ears. And your mother sends you to your room without giving you the hot chocolate she had ready and waiting for you made from bars of chocolate which she buys unsweetened so you won't be tempted to pilfer it, and you lie on the bed with your face in the pillow and your knuckles grinding into your eyes until you don't know whether you're still crying or not and you remember the story of little Billy Kryswaty: he'd been walking along the river-edge last November, he told the class, when suddenly his foot went through the ice and he slipped on the stones and went under, came up spluttering then screaming with the pain of the cold, started running down the road but his clothes sprouted icicles and grew so stiff he was forced to slow down, then it was his own body that stiffened and slowed him even more so that by the time he got home his arms and legs were completely frozen and he told the class how his father had gathered him in his arms and carried him to his bed, and how his old housekeeper since his mother was dead had very gently removed all his clothes and undone her braids and stroked his body with her long grey hair long into the night bringing it oh so gradually back to life, moving her head with the undulating waves of hair up and down over his chest back and forth over his thighs and his arms singing to him all the while in Ukrainian, and you Paddon took your fists out of your eyes and tried to imagine what it would be like to be stroked all over your body by a woman's hair and her song.

Weren't you ever happy as a child?

Yes, during vacations up at your uncle Jake's. Unfortunately Peace River Junction was more than five hundred miles by train from Anton so you only went to his place once a year in summer — in winter the railway could be blocked by snowdrifts for days on end and just getting there would have taken you a fortnight. These were also your only fond memories of Elizabeth because during the train trip the two of you, apart from arguing about everything you saw and surreptitiously kicking or nudging or scratching each other, would sometimes play together out of sheer desperate boredom, games such as cat's cradle or I spy or trying to count the cars of a train flashing past by watching the involuntary flicks of each other's eyes, or else you'd lurch up and down the hurtling deafening car pretending you were strangers, then accidentally on purpose bump into each other and fall in love and get married and have children and then spectacular marital quarrels.

Jake's wife had the same name as your mother, Mildred, only everyone called her Millie and she was smaller and more vivacious than your mother — I imagine her sitting out back, shelling peas from the garden into her apron and chattering up a storm. I have no idea where your father went or what he did during those endless northern summer afternoons while the women chattered and picked and shelled and pickled and canned and you and Jake went off fishing together. You almost never caught anything but the rods gave you an excuse to sit on the pier and talk or not talk and revel in each other's company, and on the way back you would pick saskatoons or gooseberries for Aunt Millie to bake into a pie, or else just pluck raspberries from the bush for your own guilty selfish pleasure, pulling them swiftly but gently from their green crowns so as not to squash them and leave stains, feeling them fall into your hands and swallowing their bittersweet red tears while greedily pulling off the next ones, scratching your legs amidst the brambles and the

65

thistle and wild roses, yes, dogwood roses, those prickly pink Alberta eglantines a whiff of which would forever afterwards revive in you this itchy bliss, this bothering of the bees and sometimes their indignant stinging as you picked a bunch of wildflowers for your mother — not roses, not tiger lilies, but dandelions because you thought they were the loveliest flowers in the world with their perfect yellow sunshape and their kiss of golden dust beneath your chin and their magical floating stars of cotton which you puffed away to know what time it was, until she told you they were weeds.

In July that far north it didn't get dark until nearly midnight — this was paradise, you thought. Peace River country was a jungle compared with your barren wind-mauled ranch, and Jake and Millie had what surely was one of the biggest gardens in the universe. You revelled in walking up and down its rows with the seed packets slipped over the stakes saying what was planted there, cucumbers and beans, lettuce and Swiss chard, peas and sweet peas, pumpkins and potatoes, best of all those tiny bright orange carrots you could drag from the black earth, brush off and bite into directly without even washing them if the women weren't looking — no, best of all the rhubarb you would deleaf and eat raw, sitting on the doorstep and dunking the long stiff pink-and-green stalks into a cup of white sugar and exulting as, in a crunch of teeth and a rush of saliva, the two violent tastes of sweet and sour warred joyously in your mouth.

Your father too had tried farming up north at one point, he and Jake had gone into it together and somehow something had not worked out, you weren't sure quite what but for some reason Jake had stayed whereas John had thrown up everything and gone off to shoot Boers for half a year and when he came back he decided to lease a ranch down south, the land was still dirt cheap and he knew horses from the war and cows from back home, so before long he had got himself a fine array of brood mares and stallions and geldings and fillies and suckers, stock cattle and Hereford bulls, and the *S* Sterling brand was building itself a bit of a reputation.

Burned into the flesh of your brain was the image of a cow being branded — poor baby Paddon you must have been less than two at the time because your mommy was pregnant, how can you be sure you remember this but there you were, just high enough to see over the lower log of the corral fence, staring goggle-eyed at the struggle between one beast and four men including your father. To begin with the cow's head was tied to the fence and its huge body knocked over on one side, then the first man bound its hind legs together and hung on to that rope, the second man held on to the front leg it wasn't lying on, the third man forced its rump down and the fourth man your father your very own father Paddon approached with a smile on his face and pressed the red-hot iron steaming and sizzling into its right haunch and as you watched it snort and bellow your hair stood on end and you longed to run back to the house but you couldn't budge, couldn't tear yourself away, the same scene happened over and over and in the night it would happen once again, your father approaching with the red-hot iron and pressing it into an impotent clumsy swollen struggling body — Like it or not, you belong to me and you will be called Sterling and everything that comes out of you will be called Sterling and that is just the way it is — and he was right too because his daughter

Elizabeth whose foetal sleep he was disturbing never married and neither did his granddaughter my mother Ruthie and neither will I his great-granddaughter Paula, so all of us are condemned to being Sterlings until the day we die, *Heigh-ho a derry-o the farmer in the dell.*

The farmer beats the wife, the wife beats the child, the child beats the dog, the dog beats the cat, the cat beats the mouse . . . There isn't any cheese for the mouse so it just has to stand alone, it has no choice but to cower in a corner and cover its ears with its tiny paws and tremble greyly . . . It's all right. You can tell me, Paddon.

So this was some time later. You were in bed one night with Elizabeth deeply asleep beside you, you heard the muffled scuffling sounds of a fight coming from the kitchen and you inched your way down from the bed — it was still high so you were still small, still lowering yourself down backwards until your bare tiptoes hit the cold wood floor, step step step across the room — no Paddon, are you sure you got out of bed, are you sure it wasn't just a dream, did you see this, really see it with your own eyes, oh Paddon no, was it through the keyhole, had the door been left open a crack, could you make out the words, were they coming more clearly now, was she saying But I want it, I want to keep it, was he saying Another mouth to feed around here and we can call it quits, we'll be on the bleedin' streets like my ol' man, and she No — no — please don't do that please don't, and you had never once seen your mother in tears, you could not believe your eyes but your father was drunk and furious — had she waited for him to have a few drinks so she could break the news to him more gently, if so it had been the wrong strategy because the alcohol had turned to fire in his veins, his eyes were flaming and his mouth hissed as he grabbed her by the shoulder — no Paddon there was nothing you could do, you were too tiny, just a helpless little boy watching his father lay hands on his mother and thrust and shove, the chair slides out from under her and she finds herself on the floor — ah the ugly sound of that thud and then the surprised look on her face when she turns around and the hissing spew of words hits her in the face like spittle or vomit, all the filthy words you're not allowed to say and more, many you don't even recognize. He comes at her again but this time with his feet and he's still wearing his cowboy boots — oh Jesus Paddon is this true, didn't she usually help him take his boots off, straining and pulling at them as soon as he came in the door so he wouldn't get mud all over her fresh-swept floors, but no, there's no doubt about it — he steps over to her and still spewing from the mouth sticks a hand out to the counter to steady himself and kicks her in the belly and she doubles over holding the small roundness as if she had just caught a pass and needed to hold the football close and safe against her and run run run, only she isn't running she's just spinning away from him as fast as she can and shrieking John! John! and you've never heard sounds like that either in your mother's mouth before, they're full of blood and guts, the words whoosh out of her throat as if they came directly from her stomach but once he's started kicking her the pleasure of it gushes into him filling up his loins and he kicks again and again, into and into her belly — did you really see this Paddon — and finally your mother's cry changes, it's a totally different cry, a high-pitched cry like a loon calling out across a lake, a cry you would almost think was happy so different does it sound from the low retching moans she was making before, and with this high cry also comes the blood, she's just noticed the puddle of black-red blood on the floor beneath her, and at first you think the high cry must be because now she has to clean the floor all over again and then you don't think anything at all, your thoughts just dissolve into the same black-red and that's all you can see when you turn around and go back to your room, using the box mattress to hike yourself up onto the bed and slamming your face into the pillow next to Elizabeth's uninterrupted snores.

Did you really see it Paddon I mean maybe you only heard it and maybe they were only making love.

———◆———

Of course Scarlatti's cat, instead of walking up the keyboard, could just as easily have walked down it; it is even conceivable that it might have walked up it backwards. But even if the theme of the fugue were played backwards it would still go forward, and even if human beings always and only walked backwards they would still be moving forward in time.

We have no choice but to advance.

You're right, Paddon. There's no help for it.

———◆———

Yes I know how you met Karen. I asked you and you told me. I asked you because I'd never been able to fit the two of you together. Your dashed hopes and gnashed teeth, her numbing common sense. Your interrogations resounding into outer space, her reasonable prayers. Your gift for laughter, her systematic strained smile.

Your father had just died. After nine years of being an invalid he had finally expired in his bed, choking with bitterness over his rotten ruined ranch and the forced move to Calgary. He died in the summer of '25 and you came home from Edmonton to help your mother and Elizabeth make arrangements for the funeral and go through his things. It was then you discovered by accident, in the disorder of his papers, that John Sterling had married another woman just two years before your birth, a woman named Elizabeth. You showed the marriage certificate to Mildred and said You never told me about this, and she shrugged and said She died, and you said She died and you named your daughter after her? John was heartbroken, said Mildred, and it was the first time you had ever heard her use a word like that so perhaps she was not as cold as you had always thought; if she knew that a heart could break she must know there was such a thing as a heart so you asked How did she die? and Mildred straightened up from the chest of drawers whose contents she'd been sorting and said without looking at you There was a baby, it was too big, the midwife couldn't get it out. Elizabeth was in labour for three days, up in Peace River country, they sent for medical assistance but the nearest doctor was sixty miles of muskeg away, it was springtime and the roads were swamp despite the corduroy, so by the time he got there it was too late. The baby smothered to death in the womb and the mother was unconscious from loss of blood. Mildred paused then added, as though relishing the final horrific details, The doctor had to break its arms and legs to get it out. Elizabeth died the next day. Don't say you didn't ask me.

You stood there Paddon, stunned stupid. So your mother had

known this all along. Throughout your childhood she had known it and said nothing, ever, either to you or to Elizabeth. Was this really happening? Was it a boy or a girl? you said, not believing that somewhere in your father's past there was actually an answer to this question. A boy, said Mildred. A hefty little fella. So there was an answer. And if you asked another question there would be an answer to it too. For example you could ask if the baby boy had been named Paddon. But no you could not. Another question flashed into your brain: Was that why he went off to South Africa? Yes it was, she replied. Another lightning bolt: Was that when he started drinking? Maybe so, she replied in a that's-enough-now voice as she bent back over the chest of drawers.

The idea of feeling sorry for your father was so new to you as to be intolerable — but you could imitate him, at least this once. In a last-ditch effort at reconciliation you went out to Sal's Saloon that night, where the big gruff foul-mouthed gamblers sat around drinking ginger ale, and splurged your meagre savings on an entire bottle of anonymous under-the-counter poison.

It was well after dawn by the time you got home, too late to go to bed, and you were just about to make yourself a cup of coffee when what did you see coming up the wooden walk but a tall lithe Swedish girl with blonde braids tied up in fat knots around her head and wide-spaced eyes, you thought you must be hallucinating, her body was exactly like the plains you so adored, broad slanting planes of forehead and cheek, sharp angles of chin and nose, great expanses of flat chest, long strong bones of legs and arms, ah and that clean fine look she had as she carried the metal basket containing eight thick-glass bottles of milk with the yellowish cream risen to the top, tiny furrows forming between her blonde eyebrows with the strain, leg and arm muscles flexing beneath her cotton dress, bending down to set two bottles on your doorstep, straightening with a slightly reddened face, slightly redder as she noticed you were watching her through the mosquito screen, pushing back a wisp of blonde hair that had escaped from the fat knots, relenting finally into a smile and then a conversation — and you sensed for the first time how to talk to a woman, Paddon, you felt the urge to come upon this woman gently and ask her the questions she would want to answer, you suddenly saw that you could be just the opposite of your father, the opposite of the raunchy ranch men who sniggered and swaggered in their high-heeled boots and tossed back tumblers of whisky and belched and laughed uproariously and slapped women on the rump like horses, the opposite of men who needed whores.

From then on — despite your distaste for early rising — you were the only one up apart from the sun at six every morning when Karen came by to deliver the milk, and before long she started looking forward to seeing you behind the screen door with a breath-impeding thumping of her heart as she strode up the walk to the porch, and grew slightly clumsier, allowing the metal basket to bang against her calves and reddening even before she bent down, then setting the bottles next to the mat so lingeringly that the impatient horses stomped and the wagon-driver had to honk his horn. And it was just ten days before she agreed to come back once she had finished her rounds, Mildred having gone out in the meantime to do the shopping and Elizabeth to work at the hospital, and let you flick your tongue across her milky teeth and draw her angular strong body with the calico dress now stuck to it by sweat down onto your lap, and then followed you timidly up to your old room and let you undo the buttons and pull the dress back over her bony shoulders, and as you released her momentarily to remove your pants the image of your father flashed into your mind, your father's corpse as you had seen it on the night of your arrival, John Sterling yellow and shrivelled and especially unutterably motionless in the narrow coffin so that the second you set eyes on him you understood what death was, it was the irrevocable, the hammer-clang of time with no echo, and as you turned back towards Karen your cock rose strong and straight, harder than ever in your life before and you thought of the dirt above your father's face which was nothing but matter now, the end the dead end the absolute incontrovertible cessation of time, and you entered the woman's body as gently as you could and felt the juices pounding in your cock and your father was dead and the woman was open and trembling and wet with sweat and the juices were for making babies, they were mucus and marrow and slick fat clean bubbling life and your father was dead in the dust, he was over and done with and silent forever and ever and you gently rode her pushing into her softness until she gasped and bled and you spoke to her soothingly telling her you loved her, you worshipped her, begging her to return the next day and the next, so that before long you had set fire to the beginnings of a new life in her.

Was it really Karen, that young and burning bony body, I can see you Paddon but not her, was it really the same woman I met as a child and decided had been made cold from decades of nightly cold-cream application? Yet the dates are there — you were married in September of '25 and Frankie was born in May of '26. Was that the sin for which she spent the rest of her life atoning? She was ashamed but also proud, and her parents were ashamed and proud as well, for here she was having a shotgun wedding at age sixteen but on the other hand the person she was hitching up with was an educated man so her father made a point of not brandishing his shotgun too threateningly. For him the main thing was that Karen was getting off the farm, thereby thwarting the curse visited on the women of his family — his own mother driven to suicide by the infinite emptiness of Minnesota and his wife now in the process of drinking herself to death. He had bought himself a piece of land out in the Palliser Triangle near Medicine Hat and then been all but ruined by the drought of '22 but he kept on ploughing, tracing straight determined lines up and down his fields and struggling to pay for the water brought by train to keep them moist — for him Karen's departure meant, among other things, one less mouth to feed.

You, Paddon, probably could not stomach the image of yourself as a shirker of responsibility. And there was the blood on your mama's kitchen floor. So you bravely turned your back on the university and the universe and applied for a job teaching history in a Calgary high school and got it. Never in your worst nightmares, although your worst nightmares had not started yet, would it have crossed your mind that, one responsibility leading to another, you would remain there until your retirement exactly forty years later.

Elizabeth from afar joined Karen in her solicitude, sent a little money, prayed for your salvation, did all she could to help. In

January she returned to Alberta on furlough for the first time and was flabbergasted by all that had changed in just six years: the climate had gone crazy, summers were hot enough to melt your fingernails and winters cold enough to freeze your teeth, false prophets were preaching up a storm on the radio, six thousand farms had been abandoned in the southeast and the whole lower half of the province was being ravaged by cutworm rabbits prairie-fires hailstorms and, worst of all, windstorms whirling away precious topsoil while her own dear brother Paddon sank into oblivion and his wife grew weak and wan from nursing and lack of protein and the children scratched their lice-infested scalps until they bled. But especially you Paddon, it was especially you sitting there with your head in your hands that she talked to God about, asking Him to make you trust her and to help her to renew your faith in Him — ah she knew that it had wavered over the years, yes, knew the Lord's voice had grown faint in your soul, Karen had told her you'd begun to raise your hand against the children and sometimes against her, Karen had told her Ruthie and Frankie were beginning to be afraid of you, Karen had told her . . . But she knew you would reopen your heart to Jesus Paddon, knew that Jesus would not suffer so much as a single lamb to stray from His precious flock . . .

The Lord is my shepherd, I shall not want — she begged sweet Jesus to come to you, to enter you as He had entered her and suffuse your flesh with His pure love, He who had been made flesh, He who had suffered and died on the cross, He who had offered up His naked body to the nails and spears of unbelievers that they might be saved, He who had bled — and Elizabeth wept as she prayed, wept as she took Communion, wept with

76

love as she drank His blood, the warm and trickling salt-sweet blood of Him who had sacrificed His very body, yes merciful Lord, and Elizabeth kissed His flesh, pressing her lips against the divine wafer and holding it up to the cross, asking her darling Jesus to penetrate her and become one with her flesh, begging that He come to her, closer, closer, asking Him to let her hold Him close against her, supplicating Him to let her kiss His poor forehead on which sweat mingled with the blood oozing from holes made by the cruel thorns pricking into His skin, kiss His closed eyelids and see them flutter open, kiss His wounds and heal them, ah He is so thin so very thin, kiss the deep gash in His side, between the ribs, asking who could have done such horrendous things to His body, asking that He accept her love, that He allow her to kiss Him closer to the navel, on the flat of His beautiful stomach, asking that He let her take Him in her mouth, that He give her His Body and give, give, give her His Blood, weeping with tender joy over her Friend and Saviour, making the sign of the cross and rising up at last to sing with every ounce of strength He had imparted unto her, *Oh come all ye faithful — Christ the Lord has ris'n again — Oh come let us adore Him*, the songs came thundering from Elizabeth's chest, she stood strong and firm on the two legs God had given her and announced Christ's resurrection in a clear loud voice and begged forgiveness for your sins, oh Paddon.

One day you caught her teaching little Ruthie one of her hymns — *God sees the little sparrow fall It meets His tender view If God so loves the little things I know He loves me too* — and you interrupted, hearing your father's Bah, humbug! even as you spoke, You bet He sees it fall, you said. Elizabeth glanced up at you in surprise from the armchair in which she was cuddling your daughter. What, dear? she said. You bet He sees it fall, you repeated. He sees it fall and He just stands there watching, the sparrow splats onto the sidewalk and God lets it happen and that's the proof of His love — hah! For once your sister was shocked speechless; you were gratified by the purple blush that genuine blasphemy brought to her neck and cheeks. And you can keep your nose out of my kids' spiritual education, you added as you turned your back and stalked from the room.

Apart from these energizing moments of wrath, your strength dwindled progressively after the day of the botched book outline, seeping from you like slow blood, circulating more and more sluggishly through your system until you could scarcely speak, let alone think or read or write. A motionless polluted poison cloud was settling over your mind and you knew it was being generated by your own idea factories — but why? — clogging your thought processes and sealing you off from reality, making you more and more impervious to the pleas of Karen and Mildred and Elizabeth. And sometimes it would be too much, their worried faces and hushed voices and clasped hands and tiptoeing about, their benevolence and their prayers, the perverse pleasure they took in responding with abnegation and sweetness to your grunts and snarls — and you would feel a flat metallic disc start whirring in your head, spinning faster and faster until at last it flew off and your scream burst forth: Stop being so NICE to me! — the *nice* an electric drill ploughing upwards through the ceiling the roof the sky to ram directly into the forehead of God. When the blood had cleared from your vision your wife and children would be standing there white and shaken, looking at you, daring to neither move nor speak for fear of sparking off a new explosion, and what were these idea factories manufacturing anyway? What missiles for what war? And how had you, Paddon, explorer of Athabasca ponds and northern lights and philosophy and music — you who admired the deft discreet ways of the Indians, their swiftness and their silence and their oneness with the sky — how had you, Paddon, turned into a munitions plant?

You would cover your face in shame.

It was spring now and sometimes you would venture out-of-doors, marvelling at being able to cross the street without getting hit by a streetcar, able to spontaneously calculate the relative speed of your legs and its wheels and prevent accidents from happening, able to walk at all since walking, too, depended on the brain and why should one of this organ's capacities function when others were so crippled?

Then you stopped going out-of-doors. This was in June. For hours at a time you would sit on the living-room couch and stare at Karen and the children. Little Johnny had learned to stand up by this time and was trying to walk around the coffee-table hanging on to its edge. You watched him do it. You hated him. He was not miserable. He was not obsessed with the concept of walking, the concept of table edge, the concepts of space and movement and possibility. He was not asking himself whether he would make it around the table, whether he should turn at a right angle, whether the table existed or he existed. To him, as to Karen and Mildred and Elizabeth, the world was already self-evident. One did what had to be done. One walked around the coffee-table, one fried up a batch of potato pancakes for the fifth night in a row, one attended Tolerance meetings, one ministered to the sick and needy at Cap-Haitien. Johnny looked up at you, glowing with pride in his new accomplishment. You bashed him in the face. Ah, the relief! The sudden rush of reality! Yes the ache in your knuckles was real and the light-red blood running down his nose was real and the whole ensuing concatenation of screams was like a magnificent concert of reality.

Outside it grew lighter and inside it grew darker. Summer came and it was the worst summer of the century. The province was prostrate. You could see the kids were dirty. They were eating and breathing dust, like everyone in Alberta. You could see Karen had lost weight. Her skin was as cracked and desiccated as her father's land around Medicine Hat; the Indians had always known that part of the country was dangerously dry and should not be tampered with but the whites had been confident that God and irrigation could overcome any natural obstacle that might interfere with growing wheat, so they had torn up all the prairie grasses and planted their holy seeds. God had led them on for a while as is His wont by giving them bounty crops in '14 and '15, then pulled the rug out from under their feet and roared with laughter as He watched them scurry for cover and scrabble to survive in the midst of the dust and destruction He was hurling at them. The earth no longer having a root system to hold it together was pure shifting betrayal. Lakes and rivers shrank to nothingness. Soil disintegrated into sand and was madly spun about by the wind until the farmers gave up. Having no gasoline they took the engines out of their cars, hitched horses to the front bumpers and dragged their families to destitution in the cities.

The July days were endless and identical, one punishment after another, God just sat up there and said Wham! take that, and Wham! take that, and as you lifted hopeful heads towards the breath of coolness that wafted through your windows just before dawn He slammed the heat down on you again, like a sadistic little boy gleefully squashing and resquashing an insect that just won't die.

Karen set her jaw that summer and never unset it again. Her body soon ran out of milk for little Johnny and like thousands of other babies in the province he drank weak vegetable soup and screamed constantly with hunger and the pain of diarrhea. Ruthie and Frankie played outside at cowboys and Indians, switching roles every five minutes, killing each other and rolling in the dirt again and again and Karen scolded them because given the water shortage she could not afford to bathe them more than once a week. The prickly dark caragana hedge was all that had greened in the garden so when the sun was at its evil peak they would crawl under it and play marbles in its meagre shade, sometimes you would sit on the porch and watch them for an hour or two but they knew better than to ask you to come and join their games. One day you glanced up to scan the sky for rain and saw that it was filled with a million tiny white flakes and said to yourself Jesus Christ is it winter already? But no Paddon it wasn't snow it was grasshoppers, the children squealed with fear and ran indoors but you stood on the porch and stared woodenly as the white cloud whirled down the block, stripped every leaf from the caragana hedges and vanished as quickly as it had come.

Then God sent blackflies — a plague upon you! Then mosquitoes! Infantile paralysis! Rabbits and rust! All sorts of practical jokes. He kept reaching into His hat, pulling out one horror after another and scattering them across the countryside like confetti or free candy. You were hypnotized, Paddon. You sat there in a daze, listening to the radio and reading the newspaper as life slowed down and started turning into death.

All the news was bad, every bit of it, across the board, from the rising popularity of the Nazis in Germany to the agonizing livestock around Drumheller. Looking at aerial photos of the badlands, you loved them with a passion and wanted to cry out to them, embrace their baked caked mud with your starving aging body — they were like so many portraits of your sterile brain and you walked along its crevices, kicking your heels into the clumps of hardened dirt and convincing yourself that nothing but thistles would ever flourish there again, not a blade of grass, not the slightest shred of green, not even a cactus, and the old words and ideas were dried and dead inside of you, rolling around like tumbleweed at every gust of wind, a History of Time, hahaha, and every so often instead of sweet healing fecundating thirst-quenching rain there would be a hailstorm, and you would hold your head and rock back and forth and listen to the wind, the empty anger crashing across the deadlands and flinging hard round icy projectiles into the ground for no reason, out of pure spite, hurting and hurting and hurting yourself until from sheer exhaustion the winds died down at last, and you cast a satisfied glance at the havoc you had wreaked and fell asleep.

September arrived and by this time there was no question of your going back to work, you could scarcely put one foot in front of the other, so Karen took in sewing, she made clothes in exchange for food — a dress for a pound of flour, a shirt for half a pound of bacon, even using the flour bag to make underwear for the kids — sitting down at the Singer right after breakfast, laying little Johnny across her knees where he would be comforted by the regular movement of her skinny thighs as her feet pumped the pedal. The needle jumped up and down all day long and its whirring was like locusts in your brain Paddon, huge green clouds of insects clicking and clacking their way across the dry brown crust of your intelligence and devouring the seeds you had planted there, long before they could sprout.

Winter came, the thermometer nose-dived to fifteen below and Ruthie and Frankie, school being closed, bickered and bawled at each other all day long as the snow piled up past the window-tops. You could not shovel it. Karen shovelled it, while the baby squalled and you put your hand over its mouth so she wouldn't hear.

Then you lost track of time. Seasons, the cycles of the moon, the setting and ringing of alarm clocks, school holidays, religious holidays, newspapers flung onto the porch, newspapers piled up on the sidewalk, all of these gyrations went on around you and made as much sense to you as a movie to a bird.

You lay in bed.

You lay in bed.

You lay in bed.

You got up one day and took a flashlight and went down into the basement where the boxes you had lugged with you from house to house were stored, all your old high school papers, the notebooks in which you had copied out the soul-lifting phrases

83

of Goethe, Aristotle, Emerson, your poems and even the lyrics to a few songs you had dashed off in a burst of artiness while your dad was off at war; then you started delving into the quarries of your own research — the university books covered with the footprints of your curiosity, that active sensitive animal which had sped across the pages underlining important concepts or beautiful images and studding the margins with question marks, exclamation marks, briefly formulated queries or comparisons; pages and pages of typewritten notes for your thesis; the fully written draft of a chapter on relativity and its implications for the way modern man would think about time; another chapter devoted to Zen and whether or not time existed independently of human observation . . . your flashlight zigged and zagged across the pages until your eyesight was a blur. All of this was far superior to what you had slogged through six months earlier, infinitely sharper and faster and cleaner-slicing, and you had forgotten it. Your mind had charted out that territory, fertilized and irrigated and planted it, then allowed it to be reclaimed by desert.

You spent the entire day in the basement, digging deeper and deeper into the boxes whose cardboard was damp and frayed with age, all that was left of a man who used to be you, a man of brilliance and sharp edges, grace and wit, and you could hear the Singer whirring above your head, stopping and starting, stopping and starting as Karen patiently turned the material and stitched a sleeve, a hem, a buttonhole, and as you read dust fell from the ceiling onto your head and shoulders, and perhaps a few tears fell onto the pages Paddon, yes I think you may have wept to see the ancient dreams pointing to a future for which it was now too late. When you emerged from the dark hole of the past your hair was white with dust and your eyes were red and your nose was dripping and Karen took one look at you and stood up so fast that Johnny rolled off her lap to the floor and started to howl and she hastily bent to pick him up but what she had seen in your eyes was true and cause for celebration: you had decided to come back to earth and weather out the storm.

She did not hate you. You were surprised to see that in spite of everything Miranda did not harbour the slightest personal resentment towards you for what had transpired between your peoples such a short time before. But you hated your job more and more, the glass-eyed indifference of your students to how things got to be the way they were.

Miranda herself scarcely knew how to read and write, having revolted against the soul-murdering discipline of the mission school. It was six miles south of Gleichen, too far to walk so she had been bused back and forth for as long as she could stand it — It's a funny story about that school, she said to you one day and you braced yourself for another laugh that was going to pickle your heart with shame for your forebears. You see, us Blackfoot, we were really a tough nut to crack. The last nut but the toughest one. Because we were top dog on the prairies, fighting and hunting wherever we pleased, always winning, always warm and full of meat. We really liked our Creator Sun, we thought he was treating us just great. So when those Oblate guys came along and started learning our language so they could tell us the good news about Jesus, we thought, they can keep

85

their news! Look how poor those guys are, no women want to fuck with them and they live in rags, we're better off the way we are! We tell them if they want to pray for us, okay that's fine, they should ask their god to let us live a long long life and keep on living. The priests try to convince us we ought to be thinking about dying and suffering but we're too happy to pay them any mind! All we like is their songs — they know some great songs and we want to make up dances that go with them. So they're just starting to give up on us when the Methodists come along. These guys seem a little more normal, they got better clothes, they got wives and they know some good songs too — different ones. Before you know it they're fighting with the Catholics about who's gonna save us. Both of them tell us Don't listen to those guys, they believe in lies, they don't pray right, they're gonna end up under the ground instead of up in the sky. We got no idea what they mean but just to stop them fighting we say Okay here's a deal, you teach us new songs and we'll say prayers with both of you, how's that? We'd sing matinals with the Catholics and vespers with the Methodists, or the other way round. But instead of making them happy that just makes them mad. After a while the Methodists start bribing us with tobacco and we think Hey, that's great — tobacco *and* songs! We ask the Catholics what they got to offer and they say We offer you the Kingdom of Heaven, and for free! So we go to their church too. But they catch on pretty quick we're just faking it, we're not serious about mending our ways — especially the guys who got two or three wives, they're not serious at all — and we keep on praying to Creator Sun every morning and buying medicine bundles and going to the Sun Dance every summer just like we always did. So all the missionaries give up on us and go off to convert some easier tribe. We're just too ornery for them.

Then when my dad was a kid, about '83 or so, this young guy named Tims from the Church of England lands at Blackfoot Crossing and decides to start all over again. Right away he runs into the same problem — we're so damn happy he can't get us interested in feeling bad. So he says to himself Well you can't teach an old dog new tricks, we'll have to start with the kids, and so the next year he sets up a day school at Old Sun's Camp — that's where my dad went. Next few years, things get real bad for the natives — a bunch of girls at the Blood reserve end up setting fire to their home and somebody takes a potshot at Tims. He says all this is the devil trying to stop the heathen from flowing into the Church of God and he's not gonna give up the fight. But the fact is, less and less kids are coming to his school. And even when they do come, everything he teaches them in a few hours in the daytime gets taught out of them by their parents that same night. So he's got no choice but to make Old Sun a boarding school. That way the ministers can have the kids all to themselves ten months a year and turn them into sinners. They've got to register as many as they can because the government gives them just so much money for each student. So they drag the kids out of their skin houses and away from their parents, the farther the better, they put them in these rows of beds and desks like nothing they ever seen before, they pass out soap and toothbrushes and teach them how to sing *Jesus Loves Me*.

Well it didn't take long for those kids to start dropping dead. My Uncle Bluefeather — my dad's kid brother — he went to school the first day all dressed up for war because he heard it was a dangerous place. But they took away his leggings and his beads and his feathers and gave him a grey uniform exactly like all the others. Bluefeather was one of the kids that died in '07. Not all the kids died but about half of them did, they just couldn't get used to staying inside all day with that bad heating, no fresh air, eating porridge and potatoes and bread instead of meat, plus the well water was bad. The missionaries got scared the government would find out about all these deaths and cut their funding, so they just wrote down how many kids were registered altogether, not how many were left at the end of the year. But finally so many kids were missing they couldn't keep on having classes and they had to shut down. So by the time I started in at Old Sun it was just a day school again.

You were open-mouthed, Paddon. You let Miranda talk that day. School for you had meant freedom — first it had freed your body from Mildred's obsessive washing and watching, then it had freed your mind from the cloying constraints of Christianity. She on the other hand remembered only the ugly grey-clad bodies of the nuns telling her that from now on her name would be Miranda and she must no longer use her real name which meant Falling Star because it was impossible to pronounce, rapping rulers across her knuckles for speaking Algonkian in class and forcing her to repeat the same prayers over and over, *forgive us our trespasses — our* trespasses? — and memorize meaningless verses from the Bible. *Last of all he made one Man. Wuttàke wuckè wuckeesittin pausuck Enìn. Of red Earth. Wuch mishquòck. And call'd him Adam. Ka wesuonckgonnakaûnes Adam. Or red Earth. Tùppautea mishquòck.*

One day Miranda stuck up her hand and said, forcing her lips

88

and jaws around the English words, That not so different from what my dad tell me, he say Creator Sun pick up some mud and make a man with it, then he blow air in the nose-holes and make him alive. Sister Angelica's grey chest and cheeks puffed up with horror, she rushed from the room and returned with Father Roberts who was carrying a leather strap and he grabbed Miranda by the arm and dragged her over to the boys' side of the room and forced her to bend down over a chair with her little pagan ass sticking up in the air, and holding her dark head down with one hand he strapped her backside with the other, intoning in a slow loud voice full of harsh joy, I will not repeat the works of the Devil, I will not repeat the works of the Devil, while the boys sat there snickering in shame and terror. She was forced to copy out the Ten Commandments ten times each and this was the way she had been taught to read and to write and *to love the Lord our God with all her heart, Nitchitapi Ispumitapi apistotokiw; kit ayark atusémataw*, and *not to take His name in vain, Pinokakitchimatchis; Ispumitapi otchinikasim*, and *to honour the Sabbath for the sun worketh not on its day, Natoyé-Kristikusé pinat apawtakit*, and *to honour her father and mother that her days might be long, Kinna Ké kikrista kimissaw; karkisamitapiworsé*, and *not to kill, Pininikit matapi; pinistat karkasanitkisè*, and *not to be indecent, Pinokatichittat*, and *not to steal, Pinikamosit*, and *not to lie, Pinisayépitchit*, and *to treat her wife well and let her be her only wife*, a commandment revised especially for the polygamous Blackfoot, *Kit-opoximaw, omanist orpoximis; mina kétchitchittat*, and *not to covet the goods of others, Minatchestotakit*. And this was why she had run away from the mission school at age thirteen and been brought back in handcuffs after scratching and biting the truant officers who had banged down the door to her mother's shack and this was why she had left school after completing grade four at the age of sixteen and was still virtually illiterate at the age of thirty-two.

On your way home the day Miranda told you the story of her schooling you said to yourself, hoping it was once and for all, To ask me not to love this woman would be as preposterous as asking me to chop off my own leg. As long as no one else chopped it off, you decided, you would continue walking on it with a clear conscience. Poor Paddon. You did not yet know that God had been sharpening the axe for several years already.

You saw each other whenever it was possible and for as long as possible, your meetings were neither furtive nor hasty, they were like touching the ground after hours of flying, telling the truth after years of lying, releasing a giggle repressed through an endless morning of self-righteous sermons and earnest hymns.

How did you come to be called Falling Star? you asked her once since her birthday was not in August, and she replied a bit ruefully that her childhood name had been Shining Star because of the twinkle in her eye, but that she had grown a bit clumsy with the onset of adolescence.

You even told her about the whores up in Edmonton and when she asked you Were they native? you hesitated and then said yes because if you could not tell this person everything there would never be a person on earth to whom you could tell everything, and hoping against hope she would not kick you out and she did not but she closed her face and spoke in monosyllables for the rest of the day.

You did not meet to make love although you made love

90

among other things and all of these things were love, including the sleep and the food and the talk about your childhoods and your children and your work and, yes, your spouses, for she was not divorced though she was separated from her husband, also a white man. This white man, she told you, had made a lot of money when Dingman No. 1 was drilled in 1914 and lost most of it in the crash fifteen years later, it was he who in the course of the spectacular quarrels leading up to their separation had given her such a richly variegated vocabulary of English cusswords, but he dearly loved their daughter Dawn and the monthly allowance he sent was enough to provide food. Miranda sometimes sold her work and then she would buy something special, a bright shawl for herself or a book for Dawn or a fresh set of paints.

She did not understand your unhappiness.

She could not conceive that there should be a gap between what you wanted to do and what you did.

She could not imagine that you might be angry with or disappointed in yourself. When you would say these things she would laugh — as if you were playing all the roles in a puppet show but she could see under the curtain.

Darling dumb Paddon, she would say, what is wrong what can possibly be wrong — and indeed when you were with her nothing ever seemed the least bit wrong and all the things that you had been saving up in your mind to tell her were wrong rang whiny and self-indulgent to your own inner ears, so you stopped up your lips with one of her nipples and sucked at her dark flesh until she felt the hardness of you against her pelvic bone and eased herself gradually gradually onto you while you remained absolutely still and swooned with pleasure as she moved slowly down then up then slowly down.

She gave you the body you had never known you had, endlessly revealing to you its surfaces and plumbing its depths — not by teaching you but by loving those parts of you that had always been in brackets, locked away, cramped into numbness. When you were with her you had an unshakable sense of immunity and impunity. Upon leaving her, well yes from time to time you would be overcome with guilt but the thing was Paddon you had always felt guilty, ever since you could remember there had been a vague diffuse objectless guilt tugging at the underside of your brain, causing your thoughts to turn back upon themselves, bite their own tails, devour themselves whole. Now — now that, because of Miranda, you had encountered something like genuine happiness — you also for the first time had something to feel guilty about. Having come into contact with the miracle fountain that could wash away your imaginary guilt, make you clean and whole and fill you with serenity at long last, true guilt broke out all over your soul like suppurative sores. The contradiction sometimes caused your head to ache though you could not help wondering whether you would have loved Miranda quite so much without the pain. Occasionally you even went so far as to wish you could pray to God for advice but you knew what His answer would be and you didn't want to hear it. Miranda would scoff at you when you confessed these ruminations and misgivings — You think too much, she would say, kissing your chest undoing your shirt kissing your belly undoing your belt kissing your rising root until your love of her welled up and welled over, so full and fine that there was nothing left to say.

Very early on you saw that the gift she constantly conferred upon you was the present, but it took you several months to realize that now perhaps, just because of this, because of the unique way in which Miranda inhabited the here and now, you might be able to go back to your work on time. You told her about the ancient dusty project. Your dreams quickened on your tongue. She nodded her interest. She could hear you. Only she could hear you. You would return to work. Miranda you decided had poured the colour back into your life.

———————

Mother probably told Frankie about Miranda. I think she did, he was her older brother and he knew how to wrap her around his little finger, she could never refuse him anything — it must have been this that turned your eldest son so irrevocably against you Paddon, I cannot understand it otherwise. He decided at age seventeen that you were unforgivable: after everything Karen had done for you, all the years she had put up with your moods and caprices, your sulking and tantrums — pouring her good love into you like milk, like medicine, never stopping to wonder if she had made a mistake in soldering her destiny to yours — you had betrayed a love you did not even deserve . . . This I think Paddon is when Frankie became moralistic, when he set about denouncing the injustices of the world, when he decided that the only thing of value in life was commitment because that was the one thing of which *you* were incapable: marital commitment professional commitment political commitment, all of these were beyond your grasp. Here was history happening before your very eyes, a world war pulverizing the planet, and all you were interested in was your self-proclaimed artist divorcée mistress! Ruthie must have been consumed with guilt and anguish at having revealed your secret, haunted also by the fear that Frankie might reveal it in turn to Karen, but no, he was satisfied to seethe with contempt, watching you come home after having ostensibly gone to the library after school — ah your precious library! ah the calm and solitude you so badly needed to think your profound thoughts! that was what it really came down to, nothing but sordid screwing around — and plant a hypocritical kiss on the cheek of your all-suffering wife and then sit there and let her wait on you hand and foot while you lit into Johnny for his laziness, his hopelessly sloppy room, the hours he spent sitting in front of his math problems and staring into space . . . Grimly and silently, Frankie resolved to leave home as soon as possible and forge an existence for himself, entirely apart from yours. He made a serious attempt to join the army; unfortunately he was not quite eighteen and the Allied troops had to disembark in Normandy without him.

You came to her a few weeks later, that same summer of '44 — she was in bed, she spent more and more of her time in bed and both of you avoided commenting on this — you pressed both her hands to your lips and she asked you how Ruthie's birthday party had gone, it was a question she had been saving up to ask you, Ruthie was turning sixteen and Miranda knew you were troubled to watch your little girl's body blossoming into the body of a woman, and so you answered at some length, describing the yellow-flower party, the daffodils Karen had picked and strung in streamers that criss-crossed the hall and living room, Ruthie's bright new yellow outfit and the daffodil in her hair, the friends from school who had come over with Frank Sinatra records and danced together as slowly as they could to his phony crooning yearning Italian vibrato, and the thing that had happened in your testicles when you saw the arm of a young man possessively curved around the small of your daughter's back, and then you went on to read her the newspaper, the Allied troops were advancing inexorably across France, the liberation of Paris seemed imminent, and then you lay down next to her and stroked her smooth brown cheek, and an hour or so later she turned to you and said Paddon tell me, how did Ruthie's birthday go?

Your blood went cold and you began again, haltingly, the description of the daffodils and crooning, you were embarrassed and she could see this so she too became embarrassed even before she began to recognize details from the story and realized you had told it before and interrupted you angrily saying Stop pretending! And you stopped pretending but had no idea what to say next and so Miranda spoke and she said It's so strange, Paddon. It's like a dream of going back, you go back to where you grew up but nothing looks familiar and you get real goddamn scared.

You nodded and still you could not speak because there was no way of denying this was fearful, any physical handicap was bearable and even the slippage in her speech but not this forgetting, not this chipping away at the very foundation of intelligence, no this indeed was fearful in the extreme.

All these things you confided in Ruthie and only in Ruthie, you desperately needed to say them aloud and so you did and she took them in, took them on, tried to share their awesome burden with you, let it weigh on her heart and on her conscience, her eyes widening slightly as she discovered these unsuspected dimensions of the adult world, the pain and fear of a father she had seen for so long as omnipotent and infallible. You even confessed, to her and her alone, that a vulgar bet was *not* what had put such a strain on the family budget the year before — this incident, your informing Karen that your bank account was empty because you'd wagered that Canadian brigades would never join the fray in Italy and been proven wrong, was one of the only times your wife ever lost control in front of the children, sitting on a kitchen chair and wailing helplessly, wordlessly, with her arms hanging down her sides, because what with oil and gas and sugar and tea and coffee rationed and most of Alberta's bacon and pork and wheat being shipped overseas and two adolescent male appetites to assuage and last winter's heating bill still not paid, this was really no time for you to find yourself without a red cent in the bank. Ruthie's eyes had grown so huge and dark with reproach and she had withdrawn herself so unbearably from you, clamming up whenever you spoke to her and avoiding you day after day, that finally you took her out for a long and tear-filled walk in the course of which you explained that the money had been used for a good cause but one which Karen could not be expected to understand, namely to buy Miranda a wheelchair. Ruthie nodded and swallowed; she was learning to nod and swallow a lot.

In '46 Frankie moved out to Toronto, dragging Ruthie with him to get her away from your bad influence — but by that time, he says, it was too late. By that time, he says, you had already made her over in your image, soft and self-indulgent and amoral — That's why, he says, she wound up with two bastards and no husband, and if it hadn't been for my urging her to take typing and shorthand courses, her whole life would have been a write-off. How many times did I hear that, I who am proud to be one of the bastards in question? Uncle Frankie really hated you, Grandpa. But you had other things to worry about during those years right after the war.

You were overwhelmed by what had happened, haunted by the images of Bergen-Belsen Hiroshima Stalingrad, the bodies the bodies the bodies of little children and old men and young women and young men and old women, hundreds no thousands no millions of bodies rotting and burned or gassed or starved to death or clubbed or frozen to death or blown to bits or melted beneath the impact of invisible rays, you tried to understand and as usual when you wanted to understand something you voiced your questionings about it to Miranda, only now you never knew what had registered of the words you spoke and what had not. One day you read her an article about the extermination of the Jews and she said this was nothing but the logical outcome of the way Christians had always treated other people. You found yourself arguing with her in earnest — annoyed with her simplistic ideas, the stubborn way in which she sank her teeth into them and refused to let them go, ashamed also of being annoyed — Hitler was not a Christian, you said, his political platform had nothing to do with Christianity. Yes, said Miranda, but he grew up in the Christian world and the Christian way of thinking, the Christian way of pushing and shoving and declaring you're the best and wanting other people's land and killing everything in your way until you get it. Christians are not the only ones in history who have pushed and shoved, you said, but she abruptly changed the subject. You know the first thing the white man did when he came over here? she asked, and you heaved a sigh. He drew a straight line slash across the middle of Blackfoot land and said Okay, from now on this is called Canada and this is the United States. You had nothing to answer to that, Paddon, you shrugged your shoulders, anxious to get back to the fate of the Jews in Europe but Miranda was unstoppable. And just because they put barbed-wire fences and guards with guns all over and change the place names they can say it's theirs. This place Calgary used to be called Kootsisaw, you know that? I do know that Miranda, do you really think you have to teach it to me all over again? Her eyes began to flash and you could see that the confusion of this conversation would not dissipate but only go on thickening and darkening like molasses. I'm not teaching you, I'm explaining how Christians think. Like the North Pole. *What*? You know who discovered the North Pole, Paddon?

The way Miranda's train of thought kept switching directions made you nervous but you resolved not to show it, reminded yourself her brain was not functioning normally, took a deep breath and answered Of course I do. As a matter of fact I remember it very clearly. *You* were just knee-high to a grasshopper then but I was nine years old, and my uncle Jake called me up from Peace River and told me all about it over the phone. So who discovered it? said Miranda. Robert Peary, you answered warily, sensing a trap. You mean he was alone? Of course not. Who was with him? You sighed — was this what she wanted you to say? — He was accompanied by his Negro aide Matthew Henson and four Eskimo guides. Four what? Four Eskimo guides. You mean they were there before? Miranda asked triumphantly and you snorted in disgust. Listen, darling, you began condescendingly but she interrupted you, crossing her arms in a gesture of defiance made pathetic by its physical difficulty. You don't even know the names of those Eskimos, she said. Maybe they were going back and forth across that pole for years! And just because a white man comes along and calls it a pole he gets famous. But Miranda — now you had raised your voice a notch or two — there *is* a difference, darling. There *is* a difference between roaming all over a piece of land and making a map of it. There *is* a difference between telling stories around a campfire and writing books. You suddenly realized it sounded as if you were defending your civilization against hers; she heard it too because she didn't hesitate to pounce on you. So if you think what your people do is so terrific, why are you worrying about the Jews? For Christ's sake, Miranda, you exploded, every white man isn't like every other white man, how can you talk that way? The moment the words were out of your mouth you cringed, fearing she would lapse into wounded silence like Karen but instead she went on more obstinately than ever. All I know is, she said, we never built factories for killing people. And when I see where all your maps and books get you, I prefer not to read and write. Thanks anyhow.

There was a silence after this last enormity, and then you gathered your pride about you like royal robes, like the finely woven brightly patterned blankets of an Indian chief, you rose and, pacing up and down the room, you made a speech. Oh it was vital to you Paddon that Miranda see eye to eye with you on this issue, there was no one in the world who could grip your mental hands in theirs the way she could, it was imperative you make her see reason so you paced and perorated, paced and perorated, and after half an hour of methodically unravelling the entangled themes of democracy barbarity literacy and racism, you turned to make sure she now agreed and saw that she was fighting sleep. Her body had sagged in the wheelchair and her mouth was slack with exhaustion. Shame rushed into the cave of your brain like a red wave, washing away the brilliant theories that had briefly sparkled there. You took Miranda in your arms, she smiled as you carried her unwieldy weight to the bed and clumsily lovingly laid her down upon it, pressed your lips to her forehead and wondered, as she allowed her eyes to close, whether the two of you had only started arguing since you had stopped making love.

The next time the subject of the death camps came up she shook her head and sighed and said So much for Christianity, and so it was that somehow Paddon you had to accept the idea that there would be no more conversations between you, and that your love was somewhere else, neither in the body nor in the mind but somewhere else.

Over the next two years Miranda's past disappeared bit by bit like the shallow glistening puddles evaporating on the sand when the tide recedes, or like a drawing progressively erased by an invisible hand; had she been lucid she could only have been horrified but as it was she was able most of the time to smile, maintain her calm, and recognize you the way she recognized Dawn or her cats or her paintings, as part of the world she had once made beautiful around her. She loved it when you talked to her and she listened to you but her mind recorded almost nothing of what you said, following your words like footprints in the sand and effacing them immediately, like a wave that only advances never withdraws, she kept going forward and each second was new, brand new, not only could she no longer recall how you had met or how many years you had loved each other, she could no longer step back far enough to recapitulate the meaning of a sentence. But did she really need information or opinions or ideas in the state she was in by that time Paddon, or did she rather need the sound of your voice like wind in the poplar trees? She was quivering with life, it was pure life but was it still human life, of that you were not sure. You had begun under her aegis to write eulogies to the present, but now Miranda's present had shrunk to a pinpoint of light and the surrounding darkness dumbfounded you.

What was the minimal amount of past needed for there to be meaning?

Was that the new question?

———————————

Some days you would just have to bolt. Railroad tracks. Yes. Running on the ties. That I can see very clearly. It was important to keep your head down because the distance between ties was not perfectly regular and you were going so fast that if you missed a step you would fall flat on your face. Head down, you saw your sockless feet stuffed into gaping laceless shoes, formerly somebody's, now nobody's so yours, in the summertime it didn't matter if they had holes in them and it was summertime so you were wearing them and they flipped and flopped at each fast step. You ran. To either side of your feet were the straight steel tracks glinting in the sun, imprinting bars of cool light on your brain that remained there when you blinked. You ran. Your legs were burned brown in shorts and naked all the way to the feet, caked with scabs and mud. You watched them criss-crossing and landing on a tie at every step as though you yourself were a machine, a tiny inexhaustible train, keeping the engine stoked and the gears oiled, valves opening and closing automatically to let the air in and out, cogs and wheels going round and round in your head as you chugged across the infinite plains with the high wheat waving to your left and to your right. I think I can I think I can I think I can except that there were no hills to be gotten over in these parts, nothing but straight ahead, two thousand miles in a beeline to Toronto, elbows jerking back and back and back, stay on the track, never look back . . .

How old were you then? Eight, nine maybe.

Strangely enough, I can't see you running home again. You must have, of course, or your father would have sent a posse out after you, but try as I might I can't see the tracks going the other way, towards Anton. All I can see are the seven steps leading up to the kitchen around back. You take your shoes off to avoid a reprimand, then realize your bare feet are as dirty as your shoes. You walk into the kitchen anyway, careful not to bang the screen door, and turn to find yourself smack up against your mother's stomach, hidden behind an apron and a print dress and God knows whatall under that. Her hips are stern but she says nothing, only thrusts a dishtowel into your hand — it's your turn to dry the dishes — and five minutes later she is asking you How many times have I told you not to sling the dishtowel over your shoulder like that? Sorry, Ma, I forgot. You know, she says, when I tell you something I usually have a good reason. Sure, Ma. So what's the reason? she says. Maybe if you tell me you'll remember. Why shouldn't you sling the dishtowel over your shoulder? You hesitate, then hazard a guess — Because of germs? Elizabeth who has been listening from the front room snorts with laughter and you feel like taking the dishtowel and wrapping it round her throat and squeezing till her eyes pop from their sockets and go rolling down the hall like marbles — Yes, says your mother, but what kind of germs? This time she's got you stumped, you don't know the answer, you haven't studied the different kinds of germs at school, you shrug your shoulders guiltily and wait for the truth to out — Hair, Paddon. Do you think we want to eat off plates that have been in contact with your hair? Clearly not, of course not, and now you can distinctly feel your head bristling with a million minute strands of disease and death.

Didn't your mother ever sing to you, Paddon? No she did not. Didn't she hold you close? Only to stuff your shirttails back into your pants and tell you to stand up straight. Didn't she take you places with her? Shopping, and to church. Didn't she share anything with you? The ins and outs of bedtime prayers. First you thank God for everything you can think of, then you confess your sins, then you ask Him to bless everyone and if there weren't too many sins you can ask Him for a special favour at the end. *Nevertheless, not as I will but as Thou wilt. Amen.* Didn't she want you, Paddon? Yes she did. Didn't she love you? Yes she did.

She wanted you to play the piano, for example. She knew she had married down but she vowed to give her children an upbringing worthy of the sweet English parlour drawing-room gentility which had always been just out of her own reach, and the symbol of that gentility was the piano. She inherited it from a dead aunt who had been senile for so long she didn't even know Mildred had gone gallivanting off to the empty plains of Canada. When Mildred learned of her inheritance by mail, she sent immediately for the instrument to be shipped, ignoring your father's wrathful protestations — the shipment alone cost more than what they spent on food in a month! They didn't have running water but they were going to have accompaniment for their bleedin' hymns!

The Sterlings' was indeed the only ranch in southern Alberta to have a musical instrument more sophisticated than a copper kettle or a banjo. From then on whenever your mother complained about the house, how cramped it was for the four of you to be living in two rooms and how the roof leaked and how the walls were crawling with bedbugs, your father would retort Why don't we just live in the bleedin' piano? and that would be the end of the discussion.

It arrived jarred badly out of tune by the journey but you Paddon fell in love with it. There was no one within any reasonable distance to tune it or to give you lessons but your mother let you fool around at the keyboard to your heart's content, boasting to everyone that someday you would be the official organist of the church. This was her only indulgence towards you, it lasted until Elizabeth was four and started complaining that your music interfered with her prayers, from then on you were allowed to practise half an hour a day and not a minute longer.

Elizabeth could do no wrong. The comparisons started the day she was born, never stopped, and were invariably in her favour. You had cried a lot, she was sweet-tempered. You had made a fuss over toilet-training, she practically invented it. You squirmed and fidgeted in church, she sat with her knees together her feet together her gloved hands folded in her lap her lips pursed and her eyes focused just where they were supposed to be. You, Mildred repeatedly claimed, took after your father, you were a wild boy and she intended to whack the wildness out of you before it was too late — whereas Elizabeth, of course, took after her.

As your shy skinny body began edging its way towards puberty, your father made a valiant effort to turn you into what he thought of as a man, namely a bronco-buster. He himself having served in the King's Cavalry still rode the ranch horses every day but he wasn't stupid — no man over thirty sets his ass down on the bare back of a fresh mustang. His own body was wobbly and wasted from liquor and he had never paid much attention to yours before but suddenly he started pinching and squeezing your biceps every night, tossing great hunks of bleeding meat onto your plate and initiating you into the secrets of ranching. He forced you to hang around the corral after school and listen to him chewing the rag with the cowboys, who stood with one boot each on the bottom rail of the fence, cigarettes dangling from their lower lips as they dealt out sentences like playing-cards, the same colours and figures coming up again and again: the weather, the names of a few whores they knew out by Nose Creek, the weather, the reputation of a new bronco-buster who had just arrived in the area, the weather, the incredible number of head of cattle brought up from the States by some old Mormon, the weather, were they going to get enough rain that summer, was next winter going to be as deadly as '06; their grunts and grumbles serving less to punctuate than to enhance, complete and even illustrate their spare, inadequate words.

You were bruised by your father's attentions and found yourself, as these awkward afternoons drew to a close, longing to hear your mother's voice arching across the flat expanse of land between house and corral, summoning you to your half-hour at the piano. Turnin' him into a bleedin' sissy, your father would mutter to the other men as you sidled away, Be puttin' skirts on him next thing you know. And he would redouble his efforts to toughen you up.

The faces of your childhood friends remain obscure. I can see you losing marbles in the snow, yes. Getting into a couple of half-hearted fistfights in defence of Elizabeth — half-hearted because you privately agreed with the insults that had been hurled at her, and were beginning to loathe physical contact of any kind. Ice-skating on the river with a red-cheeked green-eyed girl who kept trying to hold your hand. Tobogganing down the riverbank on an old flattened cardboard box because your parents couldn't afford to buy you a sled. But the friends do not materialize as individuals, they're a bobbing mass of coloured toques and scarves or a hubbub of shouts and hoots around the swimming-hole and always I seem to see you at a distance, gazing askance at the group, both critical and shy. Yes I think from the beginning you tended to choose aloofness so as not to feel left out, shielding yourself as best you could from the incursions of your prattling tattle-tale of a sister, and valuing books over human beings as soon as you could read.

In '07 your entire class would dash off as soon as school was out to stand along the road from Calgary and watch the poles being driven into the hard ground at regular intervals by strong men — ah the trees stripped of their branches and smoothed into cylinders, the silent forests chopped down and turned into pillars of communication, the men stringing wires like dull dark garlands from one pole to the next and to the next, decorating the face of Alberta like a sombre Christmas tree . . . The poles came closer and closer to Anton, closer and closer to the ranch, and finally the wires were hooked up to the house and the miracle occurred, your father summoned the family to watch him insert his grimy swollen index finger into the metallic dial, twirl the zero and ask for a number in Peace River. Thirty seconds later the instrument jangled thrillingly and Jake was on the phone. You Paddon took the heavy black receiver into your little hands, held it incredulously to your ear, strained and then, your heart skipping a beat, recognized through the crackling wire the voice of your beloved uncle. (Eighty years later you would tell me there was no technological feat that impressed you more. Not the airplane, not television, not the atom bomb, not laser surgery. This, the telephone, would forever set you shaking your head in admiration. To be able to touch a few buttons and hear, instantaneously, the real live voice of your own sweet Paula sitting there twenty-five hundred miles away in Montreal and laughing at your jokes — what could be more miraculous than that?)

Jake called every Sunday from then on. It was something to look forward to at the end of that stifling day on which you were forbidden everything, making noise and running up and down the back steps and laughing too loudly and looking like you were having fun. Jake always asked to speak to the children, and spoke longer to you than to anyone else. In May '09 he kept you on the phone for half an hour with a dramatic account of Peary's expedition to the North Pole, you closed your eyes and let his voice pour into you the shifting dangerous half-melted floes and the god-awful blizzards that made the air itself opaque, the Eskimos shouting over the roar of wind and pointing the way, the huskies dying in their tracks, the sun glancing on sheets of white so brilliant it could blind you, the sleds freezing stuck in ice overnight, Peary and his Negro aide Matthew Henson pitching their tent for the hundredth time and breaking twigs for the fire with senseless hands so that Peary could study his maps and Henson could wonder why the hell his boss wasn't content with his fancy heated apartment in New York City. These guys mus' be crazy, he said to himself, shaking his head. Ain't bad enough they drag us all the way from Africa, I bet they plannin' to build a city for us right up heah at the North Pole in hopes we finally gohn to get white skin.

You laughed at Jake's joke, warm with gratitude he knew you were old enough to get it.

As for God at around that time in your life . . . well, Paddon, you didn't understand Him and there was no love lost between you. You were lonely enough as it was without talking to people who never bothered to reply. As far as you could tell, most of what He did was debatable to say the least, and He made you keep asking for the same things over and over and usually He didn't give them to you anyway, which was pretty humiliating. You preferred a straight answer, like your father's blow to the ear when you asked if you could have a copy of *Tom Sawyer* for Christmas. When you asked God for the same thing every night for the whole month of December, He kept your hopes up and in the end all you got was some long underwear and the let-down was much worse. Basically God seemed to be your mother's sentinel — since she couldn't be watching you all the time she told you He was, and that way you felt uncomfortable whenever you fiddled with your cock. It was bad enough sharing a room with your little sister and knowing she'd run and tell the minute she thought you might be up to something, but having this God guy hovering over your shoulder wherever you went, invisible and silent as a thief in the dark, really got on your nerves.

Your mother gave you the piano as a wedding present and even paid to have it delivered to your new home. It took up pretty much half the living room and the other half was occupied by your bed because, remembering how you had always lacked and yearned for privacy as a child, you had decided the only bedroom in the house would belong to the baby.

That first year teaching was a breeze and life a rollicking frolic, you forgot all about Beethoven and Mozart and learned to play honky-tonk, ragtime, the greatest hits of Wilf Carter, yanking off your necktie the minute you walked in the door, undoing your collar button and plunking yourself down at the keyboard, picking out melodies with your eyes closed and adding syncopated left-hand chords as you went along, feeling as if deep down you'd never wanted to be anything but a ramblin' gamblin' man. Sometimes Karen would climb up onto the bed behind you and dance gauchely with her big stomach, or take a pillow and plop it over your head in the middle of a refrain so that both of you toppled backwards onto the mattress and had a pillow fight that ended in insanely passionate love-making, and no one had ever had so much fun before had they, the two of you had invented pleasure hadn't you, you silly kids.

You looked up a few of your old high school friends, most of whom were already married too and several of whom had children, and occasionally if they could get a babysitter they would come over to your place and sit around the kitchen table playing bridge, which was something your mother and Karen's mother had frowned upon so that both of you, you now discovered, had fantasized about it as a game in which two adult couples made bridges out of their bodies and somehow crossed them, but you had learned the real rules of the game up in Edmonton on your nights away from Augustine and Aquinas, and now you felt proud as hell to be sitting in your own kitchen in your own home playing a game your mother had frowned upon, staying up past midnight without having to worry about studying for exams or preparing your thesis or bothering the landlady, and what's more you had an honest-to-goodness job with an honest-to-goodness salary, not much but enough to support this honest-to-goodness wife of yours with whom you were very much in love.

Your dreams could wait, you told yourself, and little did you know how right you were: could they ever wait, those dreams of yours! Waiting was the only thing they turned out to be good at, not to say good for, and they would get lots of practice at it in the decades to come, oh yes they would become virtuoso waiters, past masters at waiting, unsurpassable if not in patience at least in pathological persistence. For the time being, though, you were doing an excellent job of convincing yourself that you'd made the right decision, immersing yourself temporarily in the real world, masterfully facing challenges, taking up the gauntlet life had thrown at your feet, behaving like a responsible husband and for once not taking refuge in unearthly harmonies and abstractions. Your wife's bulging belly was the realest thing you had ever set eyes on, and you cupped your hands around it with as much reverence as if it were the Earth itself.

Karen gave you her body as thoroughly as she scrubbed the kitchen floor. You rejoiced in the length and breadth and one-ness of it, running your fingers over the planes of her cheeks and hips and shoulder blades — it was as if she had been hewed from wood and smoothed with carpenter's tools until her angles were just perfect. She had strong knotty fingers, unabashedly big feet and a long straight nose — and she loved you Paddon with a fierce commitment that would never relax its grip, and she hummed under her breath as she cleaned the house from top to bottom in preparation for the baby's arrival.

Of course, you couldn't talk to her. Her faith was as healthy and functional as her appetite: neither voracious nor abstemious, and subject neither to speculation nor revision. It was the way it was. Requesting that she challenge what she believed was equiv-alent to requesting that she uneat what she had eaten. Like her mastication, her prayers were a swift decisive means of getting something done. Her pregnancies, as well, she handled with stu-pefying efficiency. They lasted the right amount of time, began without vomiting and ended without screams. The first resulted in a boy and the second, two years later, in a girl. Both children were born at home — Frankie came out yelling and bright red, furiously waving his tiny arms and legs as if to prove your father's tragedy was not to be repeated. Ruthie came out blue and still and, despite energetic rubbing and massaging, it was all the Indian midwife could do to convince her to hang on to life for dear life until the doctor finally arrived.

It was between the two births, in 1927, that Elizabeth left for Haiti, wielding a registered nurse's degree and a camera like a Crusader's sword and shield. Her reason for choosing Haiti would become a standing joke in the family, especially once the family had a few Haitians added to it. One day, poring over the church literature on underdeveloped countries, she had come across a description of Port-au-Prince and it sounded so terrible — what with the infant mortality rate the crass poverty and hunger the rampant superstition the political turmoil — that she thought it might be just the place for her to witness. Then in another brochure a few days later she came across a description of Haiti. What a miserable country! High infant mortality illiteracy wide-spread starvation hopeless economic situation black magic. Maybe *that* was where she should go, and not to Port-au-Prince! When she brought the dilemma before her priest at confession and he explained that Port-au-Prince was neither more nor less than the capital city of Haiti, she jumped for joy — now she knew for certain where God wanted her to go!

Having since high school read virtually nothing but medical textbooks and the Bible, Elizabeth's notions of history and geography were rudimentary to say the least. She was genuinely surprised when you informed her that Haiti was none other than the island of Santo Domingo, formerly Hispaniola, the very first lump of land on which Christopher Columbus had established a colony in the New World. No, she protested, that can't be! Columbus discovered Indians, everyone knows that — whereas Haiti is peopled by blacks!

You shrugged your shoulders and your sister disappeared, singing, into the Tropics.

Isles of the Southern seas Deep in your coral caves Pent be each warring breeze Lulled be your restless waves He comes to reign with boundless sway And makes your wastes His great highway — and not only His highway, you said to yourself, but also His banks, to say nothing of His airports and His baseball factories . . . Haiti happened to be occupied at the time by the U.S. Marines, so there were plenty of people around to translate for Elizabeth until she learned Creole.

Karen nursed each child for six months and then weaned them expertly and you watched your wife, the body of your wife, expand and contract, expand and contract, in awe of it, in awe of the whole thing, the warm tight darkness you had so gently penetrated exploding with roils of blood and wails of babies, such force of life, such spectacular solar strength, and the breasts you had practically had to look for that first summer day, they were so flat and sweet like golden low-lying hills, now heaved and hung and dangled and dripped with milk, then flattened out again, then swelled and oh the aureola burst like soft dark fireworks around the nipple and the nipple was huge and nubbled, much bigger and rougher than Ruthie's tiny passive flower-edged lips. You were in awe of her Paddon, and she still wasn't twenty by the time these two births were over and done with and her angles had all reappeared in the right places and the bottom fell out of the stock market.

It was nearly summer again, you discovered to your dismay, and it didn't look like God was going to be in a better mood this year than He had the year before or the year before that or the year before that. You had conversations with Karen that lasted long into the night, about survival. She was eager as always to help and to understand, and you knew that she and Mildred and Elizabeth were down on their knees every time your back was turned, thanking God for answering their prayers, so at last you donned the only suit you had and stared at yourself in the mirror like a stranger (your hair had not actually turned white but something worse had happened down there in the basement, some undefinable but clearly irreversible altering of your features) and went to see about getting your job back. At the high school the principal informed you that like everyone else he had been obliged to cut back expenses and had therefore enlarged the classes and reduced the number of faculty members — ah, if you had returned the year before but ah, you had not — and all that would be available in the fall was substitute work. You listened in silence to these explanations which were proffered in a kindly tone, if you told the man you had no idea how you were going to get through the summer he would never hire you again.

The utter ugliness of your situation now dawned on you. Your mother's military pension having grown woefully insufficient, she had started taking in boarders, but since they could not pay the rent she could not pay the bills and her water had just been cut off. She was living on tea and flour biscuits. She depended on you. Your wife depended on you. Your three children depended on you.

You haul sixteen tons, and what do you get — Now those sixteen ton were hanging around your neck — *haul, Paddon* — you walked down Eighth Avenue — *Haul, man* — past the soup

114

kitchens and the beggars, the rusting cars — *Haul!* — maybe the whole lot of you would end up out at the Nose Creek dump carting off spoiled food and fighting with other families over rotten potatoes and mouldy chicken bones — *Haul, man* — did you qualify for relief — would there ever be anything vaguely resembling relief again — *Keep hauling* — you could sell the piano, had scarcely touched it anyway for the past two years — *Haul* — but who would buy a piano these days — it could be sold for firewood and that was about it — maybe Karen could ask her father for a loan — no of course not, now it came back to you, his farm had collapsed the year before — you'd helped him pile his belongings into a Bennett buggy — had this really happened — had you Paddon really physically gone out there and yes it could only have been the year before but as the memory filtered back into your brain it was as impalpable as someone else's dream — let me help you see it, ah the black blizzard, yes — you were driving out towards Medicine Hat a tiny man in a tiny car, that same old beat-up Ford your mother had been so tickled to buy for herself back in '19, advancing in a perfectly straight line across the flat land dotted with nothing but one-storey farmhouses that cowered beneath the towering sky, and every now and then an empty grain elevator — Alberta Pool, United Grain Growers Ltd., Pioneer Grain Company Ltd. — like so many fingers timidly raised to plead with the sky for rain — oh that sky! that sky! it was not only above you Paddon as you crossed those bad flatlands in your tiny car, it was also to your left and to your right and in front of you and behind you, its grandeur taking your breath away, and suddenly it filled up with an expectant silence, a stifling immobility that seemed to be promising rain at last, the relief of a thunderstorm at last, and in the distance you could see a long dark crescent-shaped cloud advance across the horizon like a billowing bellowing mountain, only this cloud was loaded not with water but with dirt, and by the time you got to your father-in-law's farm three hours later God had had His fun with it, the soil was heaped like snow against the fence-posts and thickly coated every object in the house. As for the farm implements, useless these past three years, they sprawled broken and rusting on the parched earth, looking like the twisted skeletal remains of prehistoric birds who had died a violent death.

Haul, man! Your father-in-law was on the dole. You had managed to remember last summer's black blizzard but gotten no closer to preparing for the summer at hand. Your children were hungry, Paddon! And after the summer there would be another winter, and the price of fuel just to keep your bodies at body temperature rang in your head like a death-knell.

Still your wife did not complain, she was too relieved at having wrested you away from the devil, somehow you would all pull through, she told you, if you were just together, really together — sometimes she even wept for joy just to be able to recognize you again, and so those days went by, they went by all over the world, each page ripped off the calendar was a step closer to disaster and you wondered if perhaps you should stop reading the newspapers, Paddon, you wondered if perhaps your preoccupation with current events was not a form of escapism, a way of avoiding confrontation with the nitty-gritty problems of your life and losing yourself in larger issues, and God knows these were large ones indeed, there had perhaps never been issues this large before, ever, anywhere.

116

Saint Peter don't you call me 'cause I can't go I owe my soul to the company store. That fall you did the substitute teaching you were asked to do. It seemed apt. You were substitute living, too. Filling in for someone who was absent. This wasn't the real thing, you kept telling yourself. The real thing would begin some day. When the real person came back. And you went on relief, Paddon. You went down to the municipal office once a week and collected your ten dollars' worth of pogey coffee for yourself and Karen, pogey shoes and hope for your children — everything was an ersatz. Your pride had been destroyed in the basement amidst your boxes; you didn't even need to swallow it.

Patience, patience. All this had to blow over some day. It was just a matter of time. Sooner or later colour would flow back into the world. Your body would come alive again. It would, Paddon.

That winter your uncle Jake's crop up north was frozen and it was his turn to be ruined. He tried to get a job laying ties for the Northern Alberta Railway Company. And failed. He was too old. He telephoned. Can I come and stay with you folks for a while, he said, I got nothing left. Jake, you said, I just can't make ends meet as it is, man, I just can't. The line went silent except for the wheezing static of the connection. You loved that guy. The Peace River summer memories came sweeping back across the decades into you, the pier and the fishing-rods and the buzzing flies. But come on down anyway, you said, hell, we'll manage somehow — Karen was tugging at your sleeve — Two impossibilities can't be worse than one — staring at you fiercely — Uh, just a minute, Jake — you cupped your hand over the receiver and she whispered Are you crazy? and stared at you even more fiercely and didn't need to add Look at your children, will you just look — *Haul, Paddon* — they've got scabs all over their faces and necks from malnutrition — so when you uncovered the receiver it was to say Uh, listen Jake, maybe just right now is not the best time. You understand . . . There was a grunt and it was you who understood, those thirty seconds had sufficed to undo the friendship of a lifetime and you would never hear from your uncle Jake again.

———•◦•———

One day you were passing your pipe back and forth across the table and not talking just smoking tobacco as the sun slid back down its miserly winter arc at three-thirty in the afternoon and you loved her without touching her all the way to darkness. Dawn came home, she knew you by that time and manifested neither pleasure nor displeasure at seeing you, she was eight or ten and chunky with her mother's thick dark hair but a lighter skin, she pressed up at Miranda's side and said she was hungry and Miranda rose to fix her a bowl of uncooked oatmeal with brown sugar which she loved. And suddenly unexpectedly when Dawn had gone off to curl up in a corner of the bed with the cats and her bowl of cereal Miranda told you one of the stories she had been holding back for weeks. She kept your pipe in her hand the whole time she told it, gazing into its embers to keep the words burning.

He was a drunk like your dad, except it wasn't like your dad because our bodies are truly different from yours — what makes you cough and sneeze for half a week sends us stone-cold to lie under the earth, what leaves your cheeks pocked strikes us down by the hundreds, what makes you giddy and gay makes our heads crash uncontrollably, what sharpens your tongues makes us draw the knife to slit our own throats or somebody else's throat. My father inherited Chief Crowfoot's despair. He couldn't work, he didn't want to learn farming, just the idea made him sick. He loved my mom more than anything, she was ashamed to be a half-breed but her story just stirred a big anger in his heart. Then once the kids started coming it was his turn to feel ashamed. He wept to see his empty hands in front of their mouths. The kids just died and died, Paddon. In 1910 we gave up a third of our lands for permanent rations but the kids kept dying anyhow. They died of hunger, they died of the flu, one little boy even froze to death, I still remember the blue of his lips and it's a blue I can never use. No one was cold or hungry in the old skin houses but we were cold on the reservation and the only thing that could warm my dad to the bone was whisky. He started going into Gleichen which was a pretty wild place back then, showing off his gifts at straws or hands or sticks or dice in exchange for a secret shot of scotch from the cowboys, with usually a split lip or a shiner thrown into the bargain. My mom wept until no tears were left in her heart and when she buried the last child her eyes were dry as dead leaves. It was the autumn of '14, she stood at one end of the little row of crosses she planted off in a corner of the reservation, she crossed her arms and swore her husband would never come to her again.

Next spring after that the saloons got closed down by your Christian women and everything got worse. For us liquor was already illegal for many years, but now him buying it was twice as dangerous. My dad spent whole days trying to get his hands on the stuff and when he found it it was real bad, and expensive. We had nothing left, less than nothing, we were eating garbage, grass, my mom's silence would go whamming into him as soon as he walked in the door and sometimes he'd just turn around and walk out again. He couldn't look at her. He was a real proud man. Young-looking to the end. A handsome Blackfoot warrior stripped of his weapons. You know there were thousands of natives went away to fight that war in Europe. They didn't know what the fighting was about but at least they could feel strong again and die with weapons in their hands. But not my dad — he had too many kids. Only he couldn't feed them. He was trapped like a rabbit between the steel teeth of those two facts and the pain was killing him. Finally he didn't come back for seven days. The eighth day my mom started to moan. I remember she was making bannock. She stood there pushing the dough back and forth across the table and moaning. What happened that day she found out through the reservation authorities but she didn't tell us till much later. She stopped talking for a long time, I thought forever, it was at least three or four months. She was silent as the stones. More silent even because the stones aren't supposed to talk.

Miranda paused and stared into the bowl of your pipe. You did not prompt her to continue. She sighed, allowed the pause to lengthen, then ended it abruptly.

He went into one of the brothels over by Langevin Bridge, blind drunk. Demanded a woman. Slammed down some money to pay for her, most likely stolen money. The brothel owners rounded up a few friends, took him outside and pounded him to a pulp — Miranda raised her eyes to yours, got a grip on your love and lowered them again — a bloody pulp on the sidewalk.

Something that couldn't even be buried. Something that could just be scraped up the next day, hauled off to the dump and left to rot with the rusty cans.

Dawn wandered back across the room and set her empty bowl on the table. She went over to the black window and started playing with the flowery frost patterns on the pane, melting them together by pressing her fingers against them or scratching them out of shape with her nails. She was listening now. Miranda puffed on your pipe.

Before the horses came, she said, we used to go up to the mountains and make piskuns to stampede the buffalo over the cliffs. There would be lines of rock and brush in a V and we'd chase the animals in between, then suddenly start shouting and flapping our clothes at them till they panicked and ran straight for the edge. But one summer the herds refused to go over, they kept swerving away at the last minute and trotting off to safety, and the people began to starve. A young woman pleaded with the buffalo, she promised to marry one of them if they would just run off the cliff. So they did, and while the people butchered the fallen animals a huge bull jumped back up to claim her hand, then carried her off across the plains. The girl's dad saw she was missing and set out to look for her. He travelled a long time and at last he came to a wallow near a herd that was grazing. Sitting down to rest, he spotted a magpie and asked it to check and see if his daughter was with the herd, and tell her he was there. The magpie found the girl next to her sleeping husband and whispered the message in her ear. When the huge bull woke up and told the girl to fetch him some water, she took his horn and went down to the wallow. Oh, why have you come? she said to her dad. They'll kill you! But her dad told her he came to take her back. She begged him at least to wait till her husband fell asleep again, and she went back fast with the horn full of water. The bull tasted the water and snorted, There's a person close by here! He gave the danger signal to the other bulls and the whole herd rose up snorting and sniffing for the scent of the human. They rushed down to the wallow, found the man and trampled him flat, tossing him on their horns and trampling him again till you couldn't see even a small piece of his body. The girl cried out for her father — *Oh! Ah! Ni'-nah-ah! Oh! Ah! Ni'-nah-ah!* — Miranda's voice flowed deep and darkly from her throat and you did not dare look at her Paddon in this moment — but the bull said it was only fair, after all the buffalo her people had slaughtered. Still, he said, I'll give you one chance — if you can bring your father back to life, both of you may return to your people. So the young woman told the magpie to try and find a piece of her dad's body, any piece, even a tiny little bone . . . The magpie dug around in the mud with its bill and finally he found a joint of her dad's backbone and brought it to her. She put it on the ground, covered it with her robe and sang to it. When she took the robe away, her dad's body was lying there, not moving. She covered it and sang again. This time when she took the robe away her father was breathing.

Miranda's voice broke off.

I never even got the tiniest piece of bone, she said at last with a dry sigh. I was just ten when they trampled him in the earth and they never even let me try and sing him back to life.

Dawn who knew the story finally sat down at the table but did not look at the stranger who was hearing it for the first time.

Miranda patted her daughter's forearm, then knocked the cold ashes out of your pipe and handed it back to you. It was a sign for you to leave.

Another time, perhaps not the next time but the time after that as you lay in bed after loving and loving her, you asked Miranda whether the Blackfoot had believed the tales they told. She was washing her hair, bending over a metal basin filled with water she had heated on the stove, and when you asked the question she straightened suddenly to laugh, showering you with droplets — Oh, Paddon! — she stood there, breasts jiggling with laughter and water running down her shirt — No they didn't believe their religion, they danced it! That whole buffalo story is about how the *I-kun-uh'-kah-tsi* got started, the All-Comrades Society, how they got the buffalo dance. Because the bull husband was so impressed with the young girl's magic he taught her the dance and song of the buffalo and she taught it to the rest of us, how to use the medicine of a bull's head and robe, how to run the ceremony.

She bent over until her long dripping hair fell down the sides of her head and concealed her face, then started swaying back and forth, humming to herself and clapping her hands and gently stomping her feet. Looking up, she beckoned you to join her and, unwillingly abandoning the warm comfort of her blankets, you came over next to her on the wooden floor in your bare feet and gave a few tentative stomps. She did not laugh, no, she turned her back on you and continued to clap and hum for a while and then went back to washing her hair, she did not stand there and guffaw at your hairy white legs uncertainly shuffling about, she did not make fun of your teacher's shirttails and your

123

Christian clumsiness, she loved your body and her love could redeem a great deal but not your lousy dancing, so as soon as she wasn't looking you leaped into your long underwear lickety-split. Didn't you, Paddon.

You would go home just brimming with her love and it would spill over onto Karen and the children. Her love was fertile, yes like seed poured into you and burgeoning constantly into thoughts with unexpected shapes; it made you capable of putting up with anything and everything, even the Haiti-nights for which more and more women flocked each month to your living room, even Elizabeth's letters, read aloud by Karen to the tut-tuts and oh-my-goodnesses of the audience (twelve thousand Haitian agricultural workers in the Dominican Republic had just been massacred at the command of President Trujillo for not knowing how to pronounce the word *parsley*, and Elizabeth found this distressing as many of them had not been baptized), studded with famous quotes from Jesus, edifying accounts of how Western medicine abetted by God was winning out over the *bokors* and the *docteurs-feuilles*, and mellifluous poetry — *Courage brother do not stumble Though the path be dark as night There's a star to guide the humble Trust in God and do the right Tho' the road be dark and dreary And the ending out of sight Step out boldly glad or weary Trust in God and do the right* — ten years ago hearing such a poem would have made you want to roar and rush headfirst into the wall like a mad bull but Miranda saved you even from this.

Convinced that all the scars of the disaster years had now been healed, you began to write afresh, not forcing yourself to produce a book or a treatise or a thesis, just trying to trace as closely as possible the shapes of the new greenings in your mind. You wanted to write a masterpiece and lay it at Miranda's feet, drape it round her shoulders, scratch her back with it, perfume the backs of her knees with it. You expounded to her at length on the subject of time and she told you that despite her marriage she had never gotten used to white man's time, a measuring-tape that whizzed past one, divided into slits and slots and slivers but impossible to hold on to. White time was money and it flowed through grasping white hands desperate to stop it somehow, save it somehow, put it in the bank. Her people, she said, soaked in time like a warm bath, noted rhythms and cycles, sensed that in general everything was getting later and later. They did not see each day or season as a new event beginning but as the same day or season returning for a visit, a shade older than the last time they had dropped by. What was the point of cramming as many things into them as possible?

You laughed. You said you should have been born a Blackfoot.

She sat up in bed and pushed you out of her, you gasped with the shock of your disunion, your cock suddenly cold and unconnected to her but she was angry, yanking the blankets round her shoulders — I never heard you say anything so stupid, Paddon, you can be really stupid when you put your mind to it, you know that? What did I say? You should have been born a Blackfoot, you stupid idiot if you were born a Blackfoot you wouldn't be you and I wouldn't love you. You'd be a warrior. You'd have knife carvings all over your arms and scars on your chest from pulling the sacred pole with leather thongs strung through your muscles till they snapped. You'd fuck me and then my husband would kill me for fucking with you, or at least cut off my nose because he paid my parents two horses so he could be the only one to fuck me.

Your astonishment was as genuine as her anger. Miranda, you said, what are you talking about?

I'm talking about I'm sick and tired of whites feeling so guilty they destroyed us they have to say we were perfect. It's just like your Christ thing. You know, when the missionaries first went into Sarcee territory and stuck a cross in the ground where they wanted to build a church, the Sarcee were scared as rabbits. They saw this guy nailed to the cross and they said Oh oh, is that the way these guys treat their enemies? Then when the priests told them Oh no, this is our very best friend, this is the man we love the most in the whole wide world, this is the most perfect man that ever lived, the Sarcees decided they must be crazy.

You laughed but she was still offended and went on. That's just Christian guilt crap, can't you see? We were good and bad just like you guys. I'm glad I wasn't born before the whites came, I can tell you that. My mom told me about her mother, I never met her because she died before her hair turned grey, she had a life of hard misery and hard work and hard blows across the back, she gave birth every year to nothing but girls. First my mom who was half white, then another girl and another girl and another, and they all died except my mom. When the fifth one came along my mom was older and she saw her mother smothering it with a blanket. She said What are you doing? Her mother answered She'll be happier this way, I'm doing her a favour and I only wish my mother had done the same for me. So just don't joke about you should have been a Blackfoot, Paddon, I can't laugh.

You, Paddon, had once visited the Stoney reserve with your

126

Sunday school class and its bleakness had haunted you ever since.

But, you insisted, you can't mean you prefer the way things turned out?

I mean, said Miranda, I'm glad to paint and I'm sorry Dawn will never know the foothills. Why do you want things to be simple?

———————

She produced a series of strange new paintings like nothing she had ever done before, violent bright wide brushstrokes of black red violet across the canvas — but painting disturbed her now because if she stopped working on a picture for a while she would forget what she had in mind by the time she returned to it — and even the finished canvases looked foreign to her, unrecognizable within a day or two of their completion. Did I do that? she would whisper. Of course, you would tell her, isn't it beautiful? Not bad, she would say, turning away from it with a nervous shrug of her shoulder.

During the years of Miranda's deterioration the brilliance of the ideas you had given birth to in her presence was gradually dulled and their acuity blunted. You came to her even more often than before, sat at her bedside and talked yourself hoarse, describing the chaos of post-war Europe, the nuclear arms race, the invention of TV, trying to stimulate some spark of interest — or derisiveness, amusement, anger, anything — and finally one day you threw yourself to your knees and swore that if she died you would kill yourself, you had no identity without her, no reason to remain on this earth if she were to leave it, but it was too late for that declaration Paddon, and Miranda merely smiled, indulgently but absently, as a mother smiles at the excited babbling of a child to whom she is giving only half her attention.

Dawn, who was a young lady by this time and working as a secretary in her father's oil company, came in and saw you on your knees by her mother's bed and started making tea in the kitchen, handling the pots and cups as brutally as possible so that you would go away. She despised your maudlin displays of emotion.

Which was the true Miranda? you would ask yourself as you walked home — the one of ten years ago, laughing rippling confident and strong, or the one of today lying motionless, eyes fading into blankness or coming briefly into focus with a thought her hands and lips were impotent to express? Which Miranda should you believe, the one who had given you hope or the one for whom the very concept of hope was meaningless? Was the Miranda of 1937 defeated by the one of 1947? Would she not have been outraged had you conceded this defeat? So you did not concede. To the very end you kept coming back, talking to her and kneeling at her side and taking her limp unfeeling hand in your two hands and pressing it to your lips. Over and over you told her Darling I love you, I live only for you, whatever happens we'll be together and we've always been together and nothing can change that, ever. Whatever I manage to write will be our collective achievement, you are a part of me and everything I can do is thanks to you. Miranda smiled and you loved her so violently you thought you would go mad.

Karen was an immense comfort to you though she did not inhabit the same world. The existence of Karen the solidity of Karen the sound of her breathing next to you the shape of her bones which you knew as well as your own and above all her kindness and her steadfastness, for she really had put up with a great deal, did you huge amounts of good every day. Is that right, Paddon, have I got it right? Something like that . . .

The two of you drew even closer together after Frankie and Ruthie went East and left a gaping hole in your everyday life. One Christmas when you were missing them acutely and even Johnny's delighted crowing over a bicycle could not make the house seem full, you spent a few evenings together pasting random heaps of photographs from their childhood into carefully chronological albums and drowning in mixed emotions, surprise nostalgia regret hilarity and pain, pain at how obviously both of you had aged, how flagrantly life had robbed you of the illusion that you would be an exception to its nasty rule. What you had never imagined about aging when you were young was how humiliating it would be, how exposed and vulnerable it would make you feel, so that you ended up resenting both those who had witnessed your gradual decline and those who had not known you in your youth and would never really believe you had had one — yes this embarrassment, this strange obscenity of having only ugliness to offer the eyes of the world, this sense of shame secreted by flaccid muscles, flabby skin around the biceps neck and paunch, deep wrinkles at the eye-corners, was a crushing defeat indeed. You felt there was something outrageous in the fact that the more one gained in experience, the more one lost in beauty and strength.

The other even more disturbing revelation of the photographs had to do with how happy you had looked throughout the years of difficulty, how readily a smile used to come to your lips, how clear and confident your eyes had been, how strong and supple your body, so that in the final analysis it seemed as if

129

those must have been the best years of your life after all because at least there had been youth.

On the last evening of the Christmas holidays Karen made you a glass of hot toddy just as, before he left for the war, your mother used to do for your father on special occasions — and afterwards in bed, your head filled with drowsy drunkenness and warmth and memories and weepiness, you cuddled up to her flannel nightgown and kissed her pointed shoulder blade so obstinately that she finally turned to you. The bad years had brought you together as friends and separated you as lovers, most likely after the quagmire into which Johnny's birth had plunged you Karen had been relieved not to run the risk of pregnancy again — is this right, Paddon, is this the way it was? In any case she tended to act as though her body had served its purpose, gotten her safely through the exhausting duties imposed on her by its sex, and now deserved its rest.

Finally the day came, the one that had been coming for so long; it was a day in February, a day of Chinook. The unmistakable white line arched distinctly across the dark-grey western sky like a black-and-white rainbow — God's apology not for the Flood but for the twenty-below weather of the past few days: I won't ever do it again, I promise, this is my covenant with the people of southern Alberta, no more foul weather, no more blizzards, here's the arch to prove it, and here's some fine warm wind to melt all that snow I sent you, I was just pretending, don't worry, the earth is still there, the grass will turn green again and the flowers will blossom, everything's okay, it's all over now, I know things looked pretty bad for a while there but I was just kidding, it will always be spring from now on, I promise you, no more tricks, really, look, nothing up my sleeve but warm winds, and on that day in February 1950 you knocked at the door to Miranda's shed and a white man opened it and you knew he was her husband and she was dead.

She had of course left no written indication of her dying wishes but Dawn insisted that her mother had always wanted to be buried on the reserve, in the same corner plot as her baby brothers and sisters, without a coffin so that her body could go back to the earth since the whites had long ago outlawed the Blackfoot custom of wrapping corpses in animal hides and strapping them to the lower branches of trees.

They left you with her for a while, Paddon. You stared hard at her and realized she had grown ugly, her body was fat and her face was swollen, swarthy, almost purple. You turned your back and whispered I love you, and it rang hollow so you whispered it again, louder, then added her name at the end I love you Miranda, and the sentence rang hollow so you said I made you a promise and I'm going to keep that promise you'll see you'll see, and no matter what you said or how many times you said it it rang hollow. You did not stay long in the shed in which you'd spent so many mornings and afternoons, and once you had walked out of it you never set foot in it again. That night the temperatures plunged back down to zero and the foolish gullible buds which had taken God's word at face value and come out to greet the spring froze to death and God laughed and laughed and slapped His thigh, He always played the same joke on southern Alberta, winter after winter, and the plants and trees always fell for it and He always got the same fantastic kick out of it.

Of course your suicide was not going to be easy on Karen.

She counted on you more than ever before, having still not gotten over the departure of Frankie and Ruthie four years earlier, she spent hours every evening discussing her fears and anxieties with you — Johnny was going on eighteen and she could not help wondering what would become of him, he was such a dreamer, already he had failed two grades at school and did not seem to take a serious interest in anything, he spent far too much time alone in his room or else out biking along the river and always he wore the same faint smile on his lovely face, would he ever pull himself together? Your suicide would not be easy on him, either, just when he most needed a model of stick-to-it-iveness and strength.

Perhaps you should wait until his flight into life had been safely launched, until you were sure he would be able to fend for himself.

But then Karen would be utterly alone.

Well she had friends, her prayer groups charity drives and bridge clubs had proliferated in recent years, and her faith in God would stand her in good stead.

So a new resolve was made: as soon as Johnny could support himself you would keep your promise to Miranda and commit suicide. And every morning upon awakening you passionately renewed this exhilarating vow.

But when Johnny finally left home in 1953 it was not for a full-time job with an oil company, it was just to pick apples in the Okanagan Valley for the summer and then to see where his lucky star would lead him, and by the time he landed a real job pumping gas down in Kamloops it was 1954 and Ruthie was calling collect from Toronto to tell you she was pregnant. She claimed though this was false to have no idea who the father was, because and this was true she had been crashing at every beatnik pad in town — besides, she added, just because she knew who the mother was didn't mean it was more her fault than his — and she needed money for an abortion. Karen became hysterical and held out the phone to you at arm's length as though it were a snake and screamed This is your daughter Paddon this is your daughter, you're responsible for this and you stared at her in astonishment and said to yourself So she's known about it all along, Frankie must have told her before he left, and then dismissed this idea as ridiculous and pried your wife's rigid fingers from the receiver and held it to your ear; your Ruthie your darling Ruthie your favourite child was equally hysterical at the other end of the line and you felt your love for her surge up from the depths of your stomach to form an enormous lump in your throat as she begged you to send her some money to get rid of this child, this child that was nothing but a stupid accident, this child that was going to ruin her entire existence, this child, your first grandchild, there was a child . . . And so you began to speak very slowly Paddon, very gently to dissolve the lump in your throat and calm your daughter's anguish, and hanging on to that telephone you suddenly realized that Miranda had never once acquiesced in your promise to her, never once suggested that a life should be taken in her honour, besides you were now more than half a century old and suicide, like playing the mandolin under a balcony, was a gesture whose romanticism grew distinctly ludicrous with age, and now another life was in the balance and you remembered your other promise, to finish your book, the child of your heart and brain, and you saw that not finishing it would be as unforgivable as hitting Johnny, bringing something into the world and then mistreating it. All of this rushed across your mind as Ruthie's sobs flowed through the telephone wires, and somehow the child in her womb became a new chance for you, like the rebirth of time itself, a chance to do things right at last, to make up for that poor little rose Miranda had nipped in the bud, to love someone from the very beginning and never once hurt them or abandon them or lie to them, and also a chance to put your ideas in order and clean up the manuscript, to prove you really had learned something from Miranda — that there *was* no split between mind and body, that the presence of a child could foster rather than frustrate creativity — and you said Ruthie Ruthie, let that kid come into the world, we'll manage somehow sweetheart, we'll take care of it until you feel ready but please don't slam the door in its face! Please!

And so it was Paddon that you became the father of a grandson, just two years after your youngest child had finally left home. Ruthie arrived by train with the screaming bundle and you met her at the CP station and your heart seized up as you looked at her and realized that from now on there would be things too intimate for you to share, a father could not tell his daughter about his plans to commit suicide and a daughter could not tell her father about the way men had used her body, such things between you could never never be put into words, only guessed at through hints such as dark glasses or a new tension around the shoulders, only comforted in a general way with hand on hand or kiss on cheek.

Then she left again.

The condition for little Michael coming to Calgary, Karen had stipulated, was that it not entail more work for her. She was getting on in years, the litheness had been kneaded out of her flesh and her joints had grown a little stiff — her beauty wasn't permanently lost yet, only intermittently so; she had reached that critical age at which one oscillates between youth and the opposite of youth, looking one moment alert and juvenile and giving you a gasping glimpse of the girl she once had been, only to slump the next moment into a terrifying prefiguration of her death-mask — and now she began dropping hints to let you know she would not be averse to having a vacuum cleaner and a floor polisher and an automatic washer and a tumble-toss dryer too.

Since you could not afford the household appliances, this meant that as soon as you got home from work there were clean diapers to be run through the wringer and hung up on clotheslines which you had strung back and forth across the basement, dirty diapers to be rinsed — for the first time in your life you found yourself actually touching shit with your bare hands, day after day — and powdered milk to be precisely measured into a glass bottle, your hands shaking as the baby unnerved you with its wails of indignation at your patent breaking of all your secret silent resolutions. By the time supper was over and your grandson's tiny undershirts and pyjamas had been folded and your students' papers marked, you had a splitting headache and could not even dream of being so unkind to yourself as to take out your unwieldy bundles of yellowing paper. You considered getting up early to sort them out but quickly remembered that Michael woke for his first feeding at five-thirty and if you were up Karen would expect you to look after him, so it was best to get your sleep and try to squeeze in some time on the manuscript after school. If you could find all that time for Miranda, your inner voice admonished you, you should be able to find a little for yourself. But somehow your afternoons seemed distinctly shorter in the fifties than they had in the thirties or the forties. Your hope was to somehow connect what Miranda had taught you about time with your early aborted strivings in classical philosophy, but scarcely had you arrived at the library, methodically laid out the contents of your briefcase and started flipping through titles and authors in the card catalogue, than it was time to go home. Finally you decided it would be better to simply get rid of all the old work — the accumulated chapter beginnings dashing off in different directions, the efforts at outlines and prefaces and postfaces, the university papers now fully thirty years old and stuck together with mould from the humid basement floor — and start afresh, counting on the green shoots of your new thoughts being rooted in their loam. You wrenched your back making trips up and down stairs with them but insisted on lugging them out to the car yourself and driving all the way to the Nose Creek dump and shovelling them into the stink and rot. You stood there for as long as you could stand it and tried to find a reverent thought in your heart for Miranda's father, tried to feel relief that this weight had at long last been taken off your back, but your back ached more with every passing minute and you were forced to spend the entire next week in bed.

But what was a week, Paddon? You told yourself that this respite from teaching gave you time to think the project over and decide how you wanted to proceed from here.

One morning when you were a few days short of twelve, your father announced he was going to take you with him into Calgary for a special birthday treat. Just you 'n me, Paddon, just the menfolks. Wait'll you see what's cookin' in town! You tried to feel proud rather than apprehensive. Calgary was a blustery boomtown fairly bursting at the seams; its population had swollen fifteenfold since you were born, from five to seventy-five thousand, and the time had come for it to celebrate its lucky bucks. Guy Weadick — a wandering promoter who had toured Europe doing rope tricks with Buffalo Bill's Wild West Show — saw the city's potential for instant nostalgia and had no trouble scuttling up a hundred thousand dollars to throw a gigantic cowboy-and-Indian party — the Calgary Stampede, it would be called. A parade! Floats! Rides! Rodeo events! Weadick's own wife, Flores La Due, was the World Champion Lady Fancy Roper! To top it all off, an authentic old-fashioned Indian village with its quaint old wigwams was being set up in a corner of Victoria Park! You'd never seen your old man so excited. You watched him shave that morning, singing as he sharpened the razor on the strop. Had you never heard him sing before? Yes but this time he wasn't even drunk.

You drove into town in the four-horse democrat, the early September sky was overcast but thrill-seekers were pouring into Calgary by the thousands just the same, they came not only from Montana and Wyoming and Saskatchewan, which was easy, but all the way from Nevada and California and B.C. The traffic jams began several miles outside the city and by ten in the morning the noise and dust from wagon wheels were so stifling that your stomach was beginning to tense. Your father had a fresh bottle of whisky with him for the occasion, he unscrewed the cap and started taking quick sweet sips, licking his lips between swallows — but oddly enough, drinking did not have its usual effect on him that day, instead of growing somnolent and sullen he seemed increasingly elated, dragging you from one event to the next and squealing his approval — Yip, yip, yippee! Your stomach tightened and twisted, trying to tie itself into knots.

Calgary had gone mad. A quarter of a million people surged together to congratulate themselves on their health and wealth, their young strong virile brawny land, the rich lore of the West. The parade lasted the entire morning — a fantabulous re-enactment of the history of the province which, a scant seven years before, had not even been a province yet but still a part of the Northwest Territories. You stood chest-high to adults in a throng that lined both sides of Eighth Avenue twenty people thick, and all you could smell were armpits.

It started off with the Indians! You'd never seen a real live Indian before, had you Paddon? And there they were! Posed and composed, sitting on horses or standing on horse-drawn floats! Blood, Stoney, Blackfoot and Sarcee chiefs in full war regalia, their mouths sternly downturned, fantastic feather headdresses bristling all the way down their backs to the naked backs of their steeds. Strong young braves with hairless chests and buckskin leggings and red-daubed faces, armed with every weapon from knife to tomahawk and revolver to repeating-gun because this was just a game, just make-believe, they weren't really out to

138

scalp us anymore. Demure young squaws with fringed leather skirts and fancy beaded jackets, their long black braids batting gently at their breasts. All of them waved perplexedly to the crowds who had defeated them and were now tossing thousands of white Stetsons in the air to hail their illusive comeback in near delirium.

After the Indians came the pioneer missionaries, the Catholic Oblates in long brown cassocks with heavy crosses dangling round their necks, the Methodists and Baptists and Presbyterians in black and white, all of them smiling and waving their Bibles so as not to seem to be claiming credit for the miracle they had performed, passing the applause modestly along to God. Then came the Hudson's Bay Company factors and traders, advancing slowly in Red River carts and twirling beaver-pelt caps above their heads. Then those evil villains of the West, the whisky traders and smugglers, duly booed by thousands of delighted bystanders. Then the proud horses of those who had thundered in from the East to stamp out the villains, yes the North-West Mounted Police in flesh and blood, the self-same silver-templed veterans of those historic heroic moments of thirty years before. Then came the pioneer cowmen and the ranch owners with their round-up cooks — your father barked ecstatically as familiar chuckwagons rolled past. Then the frontier stagecoaches driven by the original mailmen who stroked their grey lambchops and nodded foolishly as they weathered the storm of applause. Then the bull-whackers, the mule-skinners and the cowpunchers, then the prairie schooners carrying settlers with their families — ah it was unbearable Paddon, the procession extended up and down Eighth Avenue as far as the eye could see and you were sure it would go on wending its way past you for the rest of your life — then hundreds of mounted cowboys and cowgirls, setting off a fresh avalanche of Yip-yip-yippees and spinning white Stetsons — then more floats, one series filled with the representatives of labour unions, another depicting industrial progress, and finally a triumphant series drawn by six-horse teams and carrying groups of Calgary schoolchildren, kids your age, eyes sparkling with excitement and tiny white hands waving shyly at the crowd — the pride and joy of Alberta's future.

The rodeo events didn't get under way until after lunch, by which time your father had run into several acquaintances who were competing and forgotten all about the day being a special treat for you. He swaggered off to the arena and you followed him reluctantly.

Cowboys! Just look at those men! The sweat and sinew of them! The twine and twist of them! The chest you could bust your fist against! The muscled thighs the pointed boots the spurs with stars the holsters with pistols the hat pushed back or fallen off in the fray with the beast — ah, rodeo! A man alone in a corral with a wild young steer and a rope! Oh dance that dance! Oh twirl that lasso! Oh the man jiving bareback with a frantic arching horse, buck on buck, fuck it man that's what I call a *man*! Fine-honed hard-boned blue-jeaned bucking fucking man! And such a dust he stirs up!

You choked on the dust, Paddon. You coughed and spat between your legs, under the bleachers, hoping your father would not notice but he was oblivious. And in the darker corners of the fairgrounds under the wagons around back of the saloons the young squaws were being mounted too like mustangs — did you see this Paddon, perhaps you only sensed it as the afternoon gradually thickened into nightmare, the crowd getting denser and drunker, the air growing leaden with the stench of beer and whisky and the threat of oncoming rain, perhaps you only sensed that there was another wildness being tamed, another beauty being broken, other strong young bodies bucking madly, rearing up in indignant pain and fear, their eyes rolling back as their freedom was pulverized beneath the driving hard white bodies of panting men while others watched and cheered them on to victory. Perhaps you only sensed this ugly sideshow in the way people kept jostling your small boy's body left and right and laughing noisily and making it impossible for you to move, to breathe, to think. Tears streamed down your cheeks and sweat down your back. The neighing of the frightened horses bunched up your guts. They were being broken, their backbones were snapping and their vertebrae splintering, the spurs were digging into their flanks and drawing blood, they screamed and jerked and writhed trying to unseat their tormentors and you could not bear the sight of it, you sneezed and wiped your runny nose on your sleeve, hiding your eyes with your arm so as not to have to see.

Indeed you did not see, Paddon, for these images are not the truth about rodeo, the truth is that the riders get thrown and trampled, their bones break and their skulls crack and this is more than half the fun, it's when this happens that the men in the bleachers know they've gotten their money's worth so why did you always only tell me about the poor horses, Paddon? They weren't so poor, they were young and sleek and muscular and the cowboys took real risks.

141

As it turned out the best cowboys were the Indians, not your father's pals at all. As it turned out a handsome young Blood by the name of Tom Three-Persons won the championship at that first Stampede Rodeo. He'd drawn Cyclone, the greatest bronc of all time, having bucked off no less than one hundred and twenty-nine riders and never once been ridden. When Tom made it across the arena on Cyclone's frenzied back, all hell broke loose. Indians galloped about, chanting and whooping, white men poured into the arena to congratulate the winner and cover him with prizes — a trophy! A thousand dollars! A medal! A brand new saddle straight from the state of Montana! A championship belt with a gold and silver buckle! Oh I can see you so clearly, Paddon. Twelve years old. Losing your father's hand and plunging into three or four minutes of icy-water panic. Finding it again and grasping it with such warm-towel relief that he shook you off in annoyance. Bewildered by the loud voices, the pushing and the stamping, the smell of rank excitement and manure, horse and human sweat, the peals of laughter, the thump of horse and human bodies in the dust, the snorting and spitting, the sight of men reeling dizzy drunk, spinning women in their arms, and finally the music, accordion and banjo, stomping boots and clapping hands, and your father dancing to the *Red River Jig* with a strange woman, a beautiful woman with crimson red lips, auburn ringlets dangling halfway down her back and ruffled fluffs of dress and petticoat, your father pressing his loins against her skirts, crushing her bosom to his chest, moving as you'd never seen him move before, whirling her round and round until you finally lost sight of him in the jumping thumping crowd, no Injuns here, just a bunch of red-faced white folks whooping it up, and there and then your stomach's knots came untied all at once and everything they had been holding down was flushed upwards, you puked and retched, spewing vomit all over the edge of the dance floor where you stood — that got your father out of the woman's arms, but fast. No matter that he hit you hard across the head to punish you for spoiling his fun; he had no choice but to take you home.

You climbed up into the democrat on weak spindly legs and he threw his jacket over you and whipped the horses into motion, cursing under his breath. As you left the fairgrounds you began to sneeze again and he burst out, For the luva God, Paddon, wot is the matter with yer, yer got a cold or wot, I go out o' my way to give yer a treat and yer go an' wreck the whole bleedin' day. I'm tellin' yer man, there won't be too many more chances, if yer want to ride broncs yer better look sharp 'cos I can't be bothered with crybabies always snufflin' in a hanky.

This lecture did nothing to alleviate the dreadful pressure in your chest and the sneezes were coming harder and faster now, great heaving-stomach sneezes that brought the bile up into your throat and nose again and again until you were desperate to get away, hide from your father, be anywhere in the world but next to him as he fumed and fulminated on the wagon seat.

All the way home you sneezed, and as soon as you entered the house you stopped.

The next day when he saw you coming home from school he ran over and grabbed you by the arm and dragged you out to the corral with him, but you started sneezing the minute you set eyes on the horses.

Next day same thing. He picked you up and threw you to the

ground in disgust. You were glad to be on the ground although the dirt in that corral was packed mighty hard and John Sterling still had enough muscle in him to cause bruises when he threw someone, but you were glad because you knew it was the end of your career as a bronco-buster, you looked up at the sky and saw it was piled high with beautiful black-and-indigo churling thunderclouds. You took a deep breath. Go play the bleedin' piano, he said. You got up and walked through the prairie wind back to the house without even dusting off the seat of your pants.

Had you broken him? From that day on he was more taciturn than ever around the house, scarcely opening his mouth at table except to mutter Bah, humbug immediately after you and Mildred and Elizabeth had sung grace. *These mercies bless, and grant that we May strengthened for Thy service be May strengthened for Thy service be God is Love, God is Love.* Bah, humbug, he would say, and John! your mother would say, and this exchange eventually took the place of the *Amen*.

Your father moped and snarled so much that your mother had no right to moods of her own; she disliked emotional display in any case, she was firm and correct and prepared to chastise you but virtually never lost her temper — the only time you saw her really fall apart was the year after the Stampede when, glancing at the society page of the newspaper onto which she was peeling carrots, she saw that the great actress Sarah Bernhardt, touring Canada with a play called *Queen Elizabeth*, was scheduled to arrive in Calgary the following week — and at the very thought of it Mildred was suddenly filled with nostalgia for Europe and England and queens and theatres and long gowns and diamond tiaras and great actresses and culture and so she set her heart on getting tickets for the show and John took one look at the ticket price and put his foot down on her heart but for once she stood up to him, pointing out that he squandered at least that sum on liquor every month, that he went into Calgary all the time but she was lucky if she got there once a year, that she had let him go to the Stampede because that was his sort of entertainment, now here at last was her sort of entertainment and why should she not be able take advantage of it, but the more she argued the more obstreperous he became, saying he was not about to let a bleedin' woman tell him what he could and could not do, how he should and should not spend the money he earned with his sweat and blood, but Mildred was the more articulate of the two, and the more eloquent she waxed the more enraged he grew at being unable to come up with a single plausible argument in response, apart from the huge and unwieldy argument of his marital authority with which he clubbed her over the head like a caveman until she dissolved in tears, saying she had not come all this distance to live with cows and her life was ruined.

Your father drank and drank and the ranch started losing money and he could no longer make his payments on the lease and there were a couple of very bad years around the house with Elizabeth down on her knees every night and every morning praying out loud for her daddy's soul; and it was during those very bad years that you felt your loins tingle for the first time and noticed the first hint of a curve through the flannel of your sister's nightgown and surprised her by kneeling down next to her on the hard wooden floor and pressing up against the bed while muttering the Lord's Prayer in unison with her and moving gently inside its rhythms and looking at that barely perceptible non-flatness out

of the corner of your eye and thinking about nothing nothing
nothing until something rose within you, something so pleasur-
able and overpowering that it caused you to blurt Amen before
the time had come.

It was also during those very bad years that you and Elizabeth
discovered Catholicism — ah there is more vomiting in this
scene Paddon, I know I'm making this up as I go along but each
time you vomit it feels perfectly true and justified, I wonder why
that is — Miss McGuire your home-room teacher had just died.
I can see her through your shyly shifting eyes: the sensuous ruf-
fles of white lace on her bosom belied by a dark brown skirt
mercilessly cinched at the waist, the soft curls at the nape of her
neck contradicted by the boots sternly buttoned to mid-calf, the
fullness of her lower lip defeated by the hand that almost always
clenched a rod. She was an Irish Catholic spinster, one of the
founding members of the tiny clapboard school in Anton and an
indefatigable militant for religious education throughout the
province, and now she had died of pneumonia so the entire student body was given a holiday to attend her funeral mass in Calgary. Neither of you had ever before set foot in a cathedral, for
Elizabeth it was to be the revelation of her calling and for you
another wince-provoking memory of shame.

Saint Mary's was made of sandstone instead of wood, it had
domes and spires and ornamental glass instead of the steep
steeples and bare walls to which you were accustomed, it was
hot and stuffy and sound bounced around inside of it confus-
ingly. The service seemed to drag on forever with troops of
choirboys dressed in long red gowns and white smocks following the priests and deacons and archdeacons decked out in

pointy jewelled hats and floor-length gowns with gold-threaded scarves draped over their shoulders, moving forward at a solemn stately pace and swinging bronze incense burners from which poured pungent clouds of smoke and intoning Latin phrases that leaned endlessly on the same note, then at the very end of the phrase went up one tone then down again and the choir and the congregation mournfully responded, always in unison, a single plaintive melody hovering around one note. This was plainsong. The coffin was in the centre aisle near the altar and to you the sickly sweetness of the flowers heaped upon it was the reek of death and so was the ominous sweetness of the incense and so was the ethereal sweetness of the boys' wavering soprano voices and so was the thick gluey sweetness of the priests' nasal chants, and as death forced its way into your nostrils the sparkling mitre jewels flashed signals like evil eyes and the incense burners swung gleaming back and forth in clouds of hell-smoke and the red and white bodies swayed frighteningly from side to side as they inched down the aisle and the organ blared forth the will of God, completely filling the air of the cathedral which was already overfull with the shifting hues of sunlight streaming through stained glass, the mounds of flowers, the crowds of mourners squeezed into pews and jostling each other for standing room at the back, the high piercing voices of the choir boys and the deep dark intonations of the priests, teeming and thronging with movement and sound and colour until finally it overflowed, spurting from your stomach onto the prayer-mat at your feet which then had to be taken home and laundered by your mortified mother and meekly returned the following week when it was dry.

In the meantime Elizabeth, after a brief consultation with God, had announced her intention to convert to Catholicism and your father had slammed his fist down so hard that the plywood table had cracked, declaring there would be no frigging supporter of the popery living under a roof he had built with his own hands, and your mother had said Now, John.

Almost overnight your heads, which had been bobbing up and down just above the poverty level, went under.

Oh she didn't mind, that Karen. She was eager to prove she had meant it when she said *For better or for worse* and intended to stoically stick by you in hard times. Her grandmother having responded to despair by stringing herself up on the rafters and her mother by guzzling home-brewed hops, she had long ago adopted her father's solution of redoubling one's efforts and trusting to God. Fortunately for you Paddon she was a miracle of husbandry and clever making-do, sewing the children's clothes herself out of castoffs — and you watched with terror as their feet grew, remembering your own summer shoes, remembering how when autumn came around your father used to fix the holes in the soles with cardboard that grew soggy when it rained, remembering the sharp bite of stones at the heel and knowing that even Karen could not make shoes. It hurt you to see the blithe lithe dairy-girl gradually turning into a Scandinavian version of your mother, scrubbing and scolding, singing brave hymns, praying for the dough to rise, pressing shirts, washing windows, rinsing diapers full of shit and falling into bed exhausted night after night.

By 1931 you realized that despite your job, despite weekly monthly and yearly budgets painstakingly planned, despite household expenses entered in a ledger to the penny, you were so deeply in debt that you could not think further back in history than last month's paycheck, which you had spent two months ago. Like the painfully tiny waist of an hourglass, your body had turned into a narrow passageway between the outside world and the needs of your family through which money had to flow.

Sometimes you would get to thinking about this and have a few drinks and one of your father's rowdy bawdy English songs would come back to you and you would bang it out on the piano and make your children shriek with laughter: *Oh, a capital ship for an ocean trip Was the* Walloping Window-Blind *No gale that blew dismayed the crew Nor troubled the captain's mind And the man at the wheel was made to feel Content at the slightest blow-ho-ho Though it often appeared when the gale had cleared That he'd been in his bunk below.* Other times you would mope around the house in frowning silence, oblivious to Frankie's and Ruthie's attempts to tickle you awake, chortle you to life again, tease you back to the sphere of their existence. They would come away crestfallen, tingling with defeat. Karen's lips would tighten — she disapproved of exhibiting one's moods in front of children — but she would say nothing, merely try to soothe them by drawing them gently into some other occupation. She was worthy of their trust; always the same. You were a dozen different men, none of them the man you wanted to be. Was it around this time that you dreamed the dream about birdsong?

A voice was urging me to come and listen to a bird singing —
it was simply marvellous, the person insisted — and I said, Yes

yes, in a minute, I'm busy just now but I'll be right there — and the voice said, But it's so gorgeous, so magnificent, this birdsong, you simply must come and hear it — and I said, Don't worry, I'm coming, I'm almost finished what I'm in the middle of doing — and the voice said, But the bird is singing NOW! And I awoke with the sinking realization that the bird was my own intelligence, and that if I did not pay attention to it now it would stop singing and eventually fly away never to return . . . When I finally do find the time, after all these years, to turn inwards and listen to the magic warbling of my mind, will there be nothing left to hear?

Meanwhile Elizabeth was thoroughly enjoying herself in Haiti. She wrote detailed letters to your mother, asking her to share them with you and Karen, about how warm and friendly the Haitian people were and what devout Catholics they already appeared to be. Quite early on she mentioned there was a bit of a problem with the pig program the Marines had set up in 1915 but it took you several months to piece together what had actually gone wrong. One of the first things these roly-poly pink-and-white human beings had done in Haiti was to introduce roly-poly pink-and-white pigs to the skinny black raggledy-taggledy peasants who up until then had been perfectly content with their skinny black raggledy-taggledy pigs, descendants of the wild boars which had run rampant on the island in its buccaneer heyday. The black pigs had loved eating garbage, they had lived in the yards and kept them spick and span by feeding on the peelings of mangoes and plantain bananas and avocados that lay about, fattening up and snoozing in the sun and playing with the children until at last they were slaughtered at the end of the year for Independence Day celebrations. The pink pigs were snobs, they turned up their snouts at Haitian garbage and refused to touch it and the poor peasants could hardly be expected to use their meagre staples of corn and beans to feed pigs when they barely and sometimes less than barely sufficed to nourish their own children with occasionally a few handfuls left over to sell at the marketplace. So the pink pigs up and died and the yards overflowed with garbage which attracted flies which spread germs which had a ball with the vulnerable bodies of the children so that more and more of them grew glass-eyed and quietly lay down and passed away. Fortunately in most cases, added Elizabeth, they had been baptized.

The letter-reading sessions were bad enough but every month or so your sister would send packets of photographs and Mildred would organize a meeting with her friends from church to look at them and feel hurt if you did not attend. She was so proud of her daughter, and of course by implicit comparison so disappointed in you, the insidious pressure was always there — be good, Paddon, you're not good enough, try a little harder, be a little better, we're all rooting for you, we're all on your side, but nothing can be had for nothing, you've got to make an effort, turn over a new leaf, take yourself in hand.

The Haitian photo get-togethers always wound up with a vibrant hymn session. The piano no longer being around to help, there was often some uncertainty as to key but never the least insufficiency of volume: *Coming coming yes they are Coming coming from afar From the wild and scorching desert Afric's sons of colour deep Jesus' love has drawn and won them At his Cross they bow and weep.* You bet they bow and weep, you said to yourself. You bet they do. Martial law had been declared in Haiti, Elizabeth

said, most of the high schools were on strike, military reinforce-
ments had been sent in from the United States and jittery
Marines had gunned down dozens of peasants, mistaking them
for demonstrators. You were furious with your sister. You
resented her praying for you like a heathen, and you resented
her praying for the heathen. You laughed maliciously when one
of her letters finally confessed dismay: these perverse people
could not stop dancing and smiling and joking and fooling
around no matter how miserable they were! Moreover it turned
out that for the Haitians Catholicism was not only compatible
but conflatable with voodoo — the more saints the better! How
could she ever hope to extirpate the devil if he went around dis-
guised as God? They pretended to be praying to the Virgin
Mary when in fact they were paying homage to Erzulie Frieda,
the goddess of erotic love! They put statues of Saint Patrick all
over the place because he had snakes around his legs and that
reminded them of the great snake-spirit Damballah! They ven-
erated the sacrificial Lamb because they themselves slit the
throats of goats and bulls and chickens, then splattered the
blood all over their heads! So, wrote Elizabeth in desperation,
you can walk into a shrine and think, Oh, that's great, these people have heard the Good News, but in fact every cross is a salu-
tation to Papa Legba, god of the crossroads, every rosary a necklace to heighten the seductiveness of Erzulie, every hymn an
invitation to possession!

The Methodist ladies were very nearly as shocked by the
Catholic rites as they were by voodoo but Mildred staunchly
defended her daughter's conversion — When you come right
down to it, she said, the important thing is bringing these poor

folks out of their darkness, now isn't it? You longed to stamp your foot and pound your fist and tell your sister For Heaven's sake, can't you see the Haitians are better off without you? — but the fact of the matter was that the evocation of Haiti's poverty in Elizabeth's letters and photographs took your breath away. You could not deny that these people needed vaccinations and bandages and food and sterilized water and that Elizabeth, whose mind cavorted in the nebulous heavens with her haloed hero, was doing something to concretely improve individual human lives on the face of this earth, while you who suffered no illusions about eternal bliss nattered on year after year about English kings and how Alexander Mackenzie had blazed a path to the Pacific.

You longed to rant and rave at your sister, demonstrating with rhetorical thunder and lightning that one myth was as valid as another — but the fact of the matter was that her photos of voodoo services made your skin crawl. How can they even breathe let alone worship in the midst of all that junk, you wondered, grimacing at the proliferation of candles and flowers and sequined flags and the libations of white flour and fried corn and liqueur — junk, junk, junk — recoiling from the images of carnival, the jiggling jumbled crowds of black bodies topped with towering headdresses and masks of fur and feather, paint and glitter — junk, junk, junk — and as you watched them dance, though the photographs were still and the room silent but for the tiny excited titters emitted by your mother's friends, you could feel the pulsation of the drums in the Haitian heat, stirring the bodies to a frenzy — junk, more junk — and your stomach would turn over as a knife passed into the throat of a live

153

chicken and the woman who was holding it deftly broke its wings — junk, junk — and your heart would seize up with fear as a man possessed by Ogoun Ferraille the war god leapt into the air and crashed to the ground, leapt and crashed, leapt and crashed until he had to be restrained — oh you looked at the photographs Paddon, yes you looked, whether out of obedience or masochism you could not tear your eyes away, but when it was over you would leave the house in a cold sweat, digging your fingernails into your palms to stave off the swells of nausea.

Your mental mayhem after evenings like this made you want to be running down the railroad tracks again, just the two straight parallel lines and the hundreds of perpendicular ties striping their way across the flats to infinity, just the huff and the puff of your own breathing and no other sound in the world, just the perfect emptiness of the plain which you absorbed and allowed to spread slowly inside you until your mind was as empty and smooth and silent as the prairies — yes Paddon, until you were not only alone but even more alone than that, until there was not even a you left to revel in your aloneness but only the song, the single singing line of notes, the one long lovely modulated plaintive melody, the endless rippling golden unadulterated plainsong.

Instead, you had to go home and get into bed next to Karen and listen to her wondering whether Ruthie was going to need braces on her teeth and cleverly planning how to save money over the next few months in the event that she did by replacing margarine with lard in her pie crusts and the next morning you had to get up early to prepare a quiz for your students on the life and death of Samuel de Champlain.

I know two things for certain about 1935. The first is more momentous than the second but far more difficult for me to see: your mother died, just after Easter.

I really don't know what to say about this, Paddon. I go to the kitchen and stare out at the familiar yet ever-shifting kaleidoscope of my neighbours' balconies and clotheslines which sometimes soothes my thoughts into place but still I cannot come up with a single convincing hypothesis. Did she die of starvation? Was she bumped off by one of her boarders for the ridiculous remains of her Victorian furniture and jewels? Perhaps she expired peacefully in her bed — though she was only sixty-five — but in that case, why should her decease be shrouded in mystery? Why should I find it harder to make up your mother's death than any other event in your life? Ruthie remembers she had to miss a day of school to attend her grandma's funeral, she says Johnny cried and made a fuss and Karen's shoulders trembled with pent-up grief but you, she said, you Paddon, my mother Ruthie said, remained quiet and dry-eyed throughout the ceremony. Elizabeth had not been able to come — Haiti was in an uproar. The Marines, after nineteen years of selflessly assisting the missions in building hospitals and eradicating superstition, had finally pulled up stakes the year before, terrorized by the swelling armies of infuriated black peasants. Besides, the trip by boat and train and train and train from Port-au-Prince to Calgary took five days at the least and more often seven, so that by the time Elizabeth got there poor Mildred would have begun to smell — but your sister sent a wire of loving comfort reminding you to thank the Lord for calling your mother to His side.

You did not argue with Karen when, the following morning over pogey coffee, she told you of her plan to use your home for the monthly Haiti meetings, now that Mildred had gone on to a better world. She had found the latest packet of photographs at your mother's place, along with a letter describing the scandalous celebration of Easter in the Haitian countryside, and invited everyone at the funeral to come over that very night.

Elizabeth had spent most of the previous springs at Cap-Haitien where the Oblate mission was located, but this year she happened to be dealing with a malaria epidemic around Léogane and was able to measure the full extent of the disaster. They're supposed to be miserable, wailed her letter, and look at them! This is Ash Wednesday, the beginning of Lent, when for seven weeks we are asked to give up something dear to us, subject ourselves to an unpleasant discipline, eat eels, get up at five, do without breakfast — anything to share a tiny portion of Christ's suffering — and what do they do? They throw a festival! Dancing and drumming, juggling and trumpeting, dressing up in outlandish costumes . . . This is a Rara band, there are hundreds of them, with members aged anywhere from six to sixty, they run up and down the mountains playing in every town and village, the women on their way to market join them, dancing for miles with heavy baskets on their heads, these people are dirt poor, many of their kids have scurvy and TB, but they can't even keep their minds on their work because of all the dancing and singing. The dancing is lewd, the words to the songs are perfectly filthy (Elizabeth's Creole was fluent by now and she sometimes regretted it) — no wonder this country is so tragically overpopulated!

Mildred's mourners crowded round your kitchen table Paddon to make sure they got a good eyeful of these terrible black sweaty-slick male and female sinners with headdresses of flowers and mirrors and towering antlers, gaudy shirts ablaze with beads and foil, rumps and torsos snakily shimmying in open sexual joy. With disappointing alacrity, however, Karen went on to the next series of photographs.

On Good Friday, she said, reading aloud from the letter, they spend the whole day acting out the story of Our Lord's betrayal. They make a giant effigy of Judas, then beat it over the head and drag it around in the dust, screaming Kill the Jew! Kill the Jew! and finally they burn it. The man you see here is playing the part of Judas. He goes crawling down the road on his hands and knees and everyone runs after him cracking whips and whooping it up — and this is supposed to be the story of Christ's Passion!

Amidst the shocked delighted oh's and ah's you sat back, Paddon, discreetly turned away from this obscene game of show-and-tell, and lit your pipe. You had taken up pipe smoking recently: biting into the hard dark stem made you feel you were getting a grip at least on something, and the burning sensation of the bowl cupped in your hand was a tiny proof of warmth somewhere. Moreover the women considered tobacco as both an extravagance and a sin, so this was your persistent mild defiance of their values.

The second thing that happened in 1935 I know for sure because Mother told me about it just the other day. A lot of details need to be filled in, though.

One night in June you stayed up late alone, maybe standing on the porch smoking and staring at the stars, yes long after Karen and the kids had gone to bed. The day's heat took hours to relinquish its iron clamp hold on the earth and shiver back into the sky, you stood there feeling it dissipate and thinking about nothing much and puffing regularly on your pipe to stave off blackflies — oh this I can see very clearly Paddon, why all of a sudden this cooling-off June night and you standing alone there on the porch with a wisp of smoke curling above your head I don't know, in any case it was probably two or three in the morning when you finally stepped back inside, pulled the screen door to — Johnny had punched holes in the mosquito screen and you could not afford a new one — walked across the kitchen linoleum which was getting dull and cracked despite the loving care lavished on it by your wife — headed towards your bedroom and suddenly changed your mind, turning right instead of left and going into the children's room. Frankie's bed was nearest the window and Johnny's nearest the door, Ruthie's was in the middle and you stood there in the dark-grey summer night and looked at these three inert but throbbing living dreaming separate products of your loins and were moved to kiss them in their sleep. As you bent over Ruthie, her head shifted and you heard a crackling of paper. Reached under her pillow and withdrew an envelope. Took it back to the kitchen and saw it was addressed in Karen's hand to Prime Minister R. B. Bennett, Ottawa. Remembered how that morning Ruthie had asked you for two cents for a stamp and you had said What on earth for, and she had said To write to Santa Claus, and you had laughed and told her That can wait a few months, honey and she had bit her lip and disappeared. Ripped open the envelope and took out a letter from your six-year-old daughter who was just learning how to spell saying Dere Mister Benet I have to write you a leter my Mother says becaus we are very poor and I need glases. I cant see what the teecher writes on the bord at school but my Daddy is unemplod and Mummy says dont bother him with this problem. Its no use it will just make him sad he cant buy your glases. So ask the leder of Canada if he can help. So Im asking you, it costs fifteen dolars for glases and we have less than no dollars she says. Please send us the mony right away because Im afraid I will faill Grade 2 and my Daddy will get mad at me.

You stood there looking at this sheet of paper beneath the naked bulb dangling over the kitchen table and you said half aloud Am I going to collapse but instead of collapsing you strode into your bedroom and flipped on the light and shook Karen awake as roughly as you could and hit her across the head and then got interested in hitting her some more because she was half-asleep and terrified and jerking about trying to avoid your blows, and also because she was so goddamn skinny and old-looking in spite of being only twenty-five so you hit her harder and harder without even telling her the reason you were hitting her especially since the reason kept changing as you hit her and the next morning, when she served them their oatmeal porridge without milk or sugar, the children saw that one of her lips was swollen and she had an ugly open bruise on her left cheekbone.

You just had to go back to work, Paddon. Fortunately you did not need to murder anyone to get your job back because old Mr. Garby obligingly had a stroke the following month when the thermometers climbed up over a hundred for the fifth year in a row so the principal called to inform you that as of September you would be back on your old wage of twenty-five dollars a week.

You never doubted a single second that she loved you or wondered whether you deserved her love or whether the jeopardy it put you in was worth the risk. Every time you went to her she stunned you, deepened you, hacked open new areas of thought in your head revealing gleaming veins of ore that had been hidden for years in dull grey rock. And you loved her all the more that you loved yourself for being able to love her so well. You loved her gruffness and her giggles, the deep creases in her forehead and the slight roughness of her fingertips, the heaviness of her breasts and hips and the sigh she heaved before she fell asleep, the darker line motherhood had left on the dark skin of her stomach between her navel and her sex. She made you weep with love, and love to weep, you who had scarcely shed a tear since the day your ears had frozen — even when your father died, even when your mother died, even when your year of time to write had come to naught.

You wept the day she told you about her grandmother although it was a very slim story indeed, a slim and common story one sentence long, a story that got repeated countless times despite the fact that it was utterly lacking in aesthetic or ethical value, the ordinary horrible story of a young Indian girl coming of age and being raped by the Hudson's Bay Company factor. It usually happened on the last day of their schooling, it was almost a tradition, part of their initiation into civilization, the priests had done what they could to whip the Bible into their pagan asses but their education was not complete until a Hudson's Bay Company factor had rent their heathen maidenheads and deposited his civilized seed in their wild wombs, it was really almost unavoidable, the only thing the girl's parents could do was to hope the seed would not flourish but the one in the womb of Miranda's grandmother had. If the child was a boy his white father would usually acknowledge him and bring him up in view of a future career as a diplomat and interpreter between traders and redskins, this was the role the Métis had been playing for the past century with a few unfortunate exceptions like Louis Riel, but if the child was a girl she was left to her fate among the savages.

Of course your being in love had not changed God's nasty disposition one whit, it had just made you stop taking it so personally. Nineteen thirty-eight was the last of the unbearable winters because by then the Almighty had gotten bored with piddling little pranks like burying year-old calves in fifty feet of snow and decided to move on to the big time. Now it was the political climate He was fucking around with and it looked like there was one hell of a storm in the offing, despite Mackenzie King's declaration upon returning from Germany the previous year that Hitler had nothing but peaceful intentions and there was no need for Canada, already overpopulated at one and a half persons per square mile, to open its doors to all those impoverished and most likely communistic and in any case Jewish Jews who were clamouring to get in, especially just now when our own employment problems were so acute. You went to

Miranda's one day in July, sick with apprehension and the need to talk it over with her, but found her impatient for you to arrive so that she could release her own emotion, which for the first time since you had met her was verging on hysteria.

She had been to Gleichen, she told you, to visit her family and learned — it was here she began to laugh, laughing until she could hardly catch her breath — that her favourite cousin Joe Crowfoot, a chief and grandson of the great chief himself, had gone to — can you believe it? Miranda hooted and guffawed — Sydney Australia! Sydney Australia, you stupidly repeated, what on earth is he doing in Sydney Australia? There's a — goddamn — rodeo down there! she gasped out between giggles. They chose — eight of the best — native champions — to go and — prance around — for a bunch of whites — on the other side of the world! You know Paddon — Miranda holding her sides with laughter lost her balance and banged into a can of paint, sending startled cats streaking into corners of the shed — they didn't just have to be — good bareback riders! They also — had to *look* like — real wild Indians! Some of the best riders — got left behind — because their noses weren't hooked enough! — Isn't that — fantastic?

This judging of people by their noses would have been a good pretext for shifting the conversation to what was going on in Europe but Miranda was totally out of your reach. For half an hour she went on a rampage of laughter-spiked sarcasm about the way the natives had been brought to rodeo. First the white man comes along and says Okay you guys, stop doing your crazy dances and your war whoops and stuff, God doesn't like those satanic shenanigans one bit and besides they make us

162

kinda nervous, especially the war part, you understand. But then things start getting dull and the white man says Well after all there was something ethnic and colourful about those customs so let's say you can do them once a year, just pretending like, in our parades and exhibitions, that way we can collect admission and everyone will be happy. And if you want to work off your excess energy come right on into the arena and ride some wild horses, you guys always have been good at mounting mustangs, and we'll give you a silver cup in exchange for the entertainment. She's right, you thought to yourself, it's exactly like the Blacks boxing in the United States. But there was no time for analogies because Miranda now was telling you — all of this had happened before she was born but her father had spoken it to her and it was all she possessed of him, this tiny piece of backbone with which she sang him back to life — about the quarrel that had gone on for years between the churches and the exhibitions, the churches saying Look we just took away their bloody tomahawks and scalps and blasphemous buffalo skulls and now you plan to give it all back to them and allow them to come off the reservations and drink and fornicate to their heart's content? — and the exhibitions saying Listen this war-dress parade is gonna draw the biggest crowds of the goddamn season! — and the churches running and tattling to the federal government about how this would defeat their efforts at civilization so that finally the Indian Act was revised making it illegal for natives to participate in fairs, and it was only when you got back home and saw Karen's frightened face as she listened to the radio that you realized you had forgotten all about the fate of Europe's Jews.

One day, a Monday early in September, Dawn answered your

knock at the door and told you Miranda was in bed, could not get up, could not see you, did not wish to see you today. She would not tell you what was wrong. You went home shaken to the bone, wondering what, worrying why, and Karen instantly noticed the change in you and you brushed her off and tried to hide behind your evening paper but your thoughts kept reverting to the shed and Dawn's impassive face in the crack of the door, then Karen turned on the radio and finally it registered, finally the message you had been reading over and over without understanding it penetrated your consciousness because of the dramatic tone in which it was announced over the radio, France and Great Britain had declared war on Germany. But what was the matter with Miranda? She had been ill before and never once refused to see you. It was the beginning of the Second World War. But what was wrong with Miranda? Johnny who was seven by this time came up to the kitchen table and started showing off his reading skills by sounding out the blaring glaring headlines of the *Herald*. You exploded for the first time in years, jumping to your feet and bellowing Shut up for Christ's sake! Is it impossible to have five minutes of peace and quiet when I get home from work? You recognized the sudden bunching-up of Karen's shoulder muscles though she did not turn away from the snap beans she was boiling on the stove, you recognized the awe in Johnny's widened eyes as he backed away from the ogre he had just recently begun to trust, you recognized the knots in your own stomach as you stalked out of the room disgusted with yourself — but what on earth could be the matter with Miranda?

The fall term had barely begun but you knew that with this

uproar in your heart you could not face your students. The following morning for the first time in almost fifteen years of teaching you drove downtown, walked into a coffee shop and called in sick, telling yourself you were sick at heart and that was reason enough, telling yourself you didn't give a damn if someone from the school phoned home during the day and your whole life fell apart, telling yourself what you believed to be the truth — that without Miranda you could not live.

Dawn would have left for school by now. You knocked softly at the door of the shed and in the ensuing silence your heart pounded as though it fully intended to batter the door down. The sky overhead was made of cobalt and the September sun of bronze — Indian summer weather, you said to yourself incongruously, wondering whether or not you had the courage to put your fist through a windowpane and open the door from the inside. The silence lasted and lasted, then you saw the latch move soundlessly and Miranda pulled open the door.

She was ashen and sullen, her chin was set, her hair was uncombed and for the first time the room's disarray seemed ominous to you. Yet upon seeing her you felt no anger, no fear, not even curiosity for the time being, nothing but relief that she was still alive. She motioned with her chin for you to sit down at the table, then sat across from you and did not speak. Neither did you. Then she spoke.

There was a child, she said, and her voice was as ashen as her skin and you understood at once and felt your hair bristle at the nape of your neck. Now you were not speechless waiting but speechless shocked. You could only repeat her words, not turning them into a question but making them yours: There was a child, and Miranda nodded. You turned away from her and your eyes were snapped to a corner of the room where a small heap of blood-stained rags confirmed the truth of her statement. You saw your mother's blood forming a pool on the wooden floor beneath her and heard her high loon cry, you stood so abruptly that your chair fell over and you whirled back to Miranda and said, but not shouting, very low, How could you? And she did not look up at you so you repeated weeping angry tears How could you — it wasn't only yours — you had no right — and still she did not look up but you could see the muscles in her jaw working and setting her chin even more stubbornly than before and so now you went over and threw yourself down on your knees and slumped between her legs as though you were the child Paddon, and buried your face in her lap, in the folds of cloth about the warm wet place from which the child would never come, and looked up at her and said, your face streaming with tears, Like your grandmother, then, you kill your own children and now it was she who stood, proudly, angrily, and said I'd rather kill my own children before they get born than hit them and shout at them once they're alive and you recoiled at the whiplash of that sentence and then crumpled completely, sobbing like a baby, sobbing with the pain of your father's blows and the shame of your own and your love for Miranda which could never become a child.

You stayed with her all that day, in mourning and exhausted. You made her tea to drink, and tried to convince her to eat something but she refused. She said she knew what was right for her to do. She had used special leaves given her by one of her cousins on the reserve who knew the old ways. Leaves only work for the first two or three weeks, her cousin had told her. After that you have to use a black bag, from the bladder of a bear. The leaves, fortunately, had been enough.

The only thing you had salvaged from the wreckage of your speculations on time was the thin blue folder from the years of Miranda's illness. You spent hours in bed rereading these flashes of ideas and trying to figure out how to connect them into a single stream of intellectual light. To your surprise, instead of leaping with fresh inspiration, your mind kept trudging along the familiar paths of mundane worries, most often involving your children. Was Johnny going to be satisfied with loafing around in a gas station for the rest of his life? And whatever would become of Ruthie now that she had turned twenty-five, broken off with her beatnik friends and given birth to an illegitimate son? The only one of your children who seemed to be carving out any sort of path for himself was Frankie, who had a doctorate in political science and was actively involved in the peace movement now trying to push its green shoots through the sinister blank blanket of the Cold War; he condescended to mail you a series of incisive articles he had published denouncing America's anti-Communist paranoia. Michael meanwhile was being taught to run home from playschool with his shirt pulled up over his mouth and nose in the event of a nuclear alert, and never oh never to eat snow because the snow came all the way down from Alaska which was right next to Russia and Russia might have deliberately contaminated it with radioactivity. *Contamination* and *radioactivity* were words your grandson learned along with cookies and orange juice and you asked yourself with a sigh what the world was coming to, wincing at the cliché even as it escaped your mental lips, sitting there with your elbows on the kitchen table and your head in your hands, ruminating about all these brand new things to fear, and because you did care about your eldest son you read as many political journals as you could get your hands on so as to have at least an informed opinion to share with him, and the more you read the more you shook your head and sighed and the less strength you could muster for thinking anything of your own.

Some days you would force yourself to write and those days were distinctly worse than the others, your sentences were clumsy, your ideas self-evident or self-contradictory, you wondered vaguely about the relation between the sentences and the ideas, and came up with some frankly jejune ways of expressing it:

> *the idea is the sentence's gift*
> *the sentence is the idea's ribbon*

Then you would grab yourself by the mental shoulders and shake yourself and say Listen, old man, you'll never arrive at any answers until your questions are clear. Just what is it you're trying to find out?

So other days you would begin by resolutely defining the mountain peak you were aiming at, then embark on a path of reflection and follow it, only to look up a while later and see that a lower but closer mountain now loomed large in front of you, totally blocking the ice-sparkling summit from your view.

> *. . . time and spirituality. The way a society's conception of time affects the philosophy it can produce, its attitude towards the*

*human soul. The way (and the reasons for which) Christianity
has lent itself to industrialization, the destruction of other cultures, war.*

*Irony: the Christians said this Earth does not matter, what
matters is the Hereafter, and the Indians said this Earth matters, it is all that matters, and the Christians took this Earth
away from the Indians.*

But does this still have anything to do with time?

Now you had argued yourself into a corner, into a dark dead
end, into a total cessation of intellectual activity, and you sat in
silence, head on arms, with no idea what to think about, what to
look forward to, what path you might embark upon from here.
Karen was so palpably anxious about what appeared to be the
symptoms of a regression to your slump of twenty-five years
before that you hastened to reassure her — No it's nothing, you
told her, I've simply decided not to force myself to write until
I've done some further reading . . .

So, Michael being a little bigger now and sleeping through
the night, you began to spend your evenings at the library again,
perusing the calendars and cosmologies of native American
tribes from the Arctic to the Amazon. You were quite taken with
these tales, and when Elizabeth came back on furlough in the
fall you told her about the Huron version of Creation — there
was a female deity known as Aataentsic, originally she lived in a
transcendent spirit world but then she fell through a hole in the
sky, either accidentally or else pushed through by her angry husband, and as she was falling the Great Tortoise saw that
Aataentsic was going to plunge into the primordial sea and
maybe drown, so Tortoise asked animals such as Beaver and
Muskrat to dive to the bottom of the ocean and bring up mud

and finally they succeeded in piling enough earth on Tortoise's back to make a soft landing-spot and a congenial dwelling-place for the mother of mankind — What do you think of that? you grinned, and your sister replied I prefer Genesis.

> *Dream in which I had decided at long last to be frank and argue with Elizabeth, draw her by force into that shivering part of myself which has to think things through for itself, stop pretending I might some day adopt her warm but stifling blanket of beliefs. Listen, I said, I'm working on the relationship between time and spirituality, the way our ideas about time affect how we think about the universe, the meaning of life. Ever since we were kids, I've been dissatisfied with words like eternal love and everlasting peace. But Paddon, replied Elizabeth, surely you're aware that the acceptance and integration of time is the central, crucial, not to say defining tenet of the doctrine of Jesus Christ!*

With a sickening feeling of recognition you realized upon awakening that there was some truth in this, and that everything you had tried to write since Miranda's death was worthless, and that you might as well scrap it and begin again.

To make matters worse it was at just about this time that Frankie decided to marry a Haitian expatriate named Clorinde, and Elizabeth berated you endlessly, Paddon, for having renounced exerting any moral influence over your children whatsoever. It was not so much the colour or origin of her nephew's bride-to-be that bothered her, but the fact that they had chosen to seal their union in an exclusively civil ceremony. Clorinde was a graduate student at law school, an adamant atheist and political activist whose feet at least apparently were as firmly planted on the ground as those of her new husband. Before long she had given birth to twin daughters, passed her bar exam and gotten an interesting though non-lucrative job representing illegal immigrants. The Toronto Sterlings set up housekeeping in a lower middle-class neighbourhood and papered the cracked walls of their home with posters and flyers and banners flaunting all the demonstrations they attended and all the noble causes they espoused. Their conversations had the same shapes and colours as the poster slogans, loud and clear and down-to-earth with a peremptory tone and squared corners, and they were determined to raise their little girls on a healthy diet of folk-songs and social consciousness. Back in Haiti, Elizabeth prayed daily and desperately for their souls.

Frankie had fashioned himself into what he considered the exact opposite of you — a man devoted to his mother faithful to his wife committed to his beliefs and doting on his daughters — so it irked him as time went on to see that Pearl and Amber refused to walk in his footsteps or indeed to manifest even the most perfunctory sort of respect or reverence for his lifestyle. They were a wild capricious pair, selfish and secretive, absolute in their passions, given to sadistic experimentation with animals and other lower forms of life such as female cousins; their anger flared readily and their grudges burned long and, worst of all, they seemed to love you Paddon more than they did their own father. As a matter of fact they were rather mad about you and each year would count the days until summer vacation when they would be able to come out West to spend a whole month with Grandpa Sterling. Clorinde always slipped a stringent list of dietary do's and don'ts into their suitcase, though the true reason for these would not come to light until a decade later, so Karen spent the better part of the day in the kitchen diligently

171

preparing the only dishes they would condescend to touch. Meanwhile you clowned and caroused with your two little café-au-lait granddaughters, watching their dark eyes shine and the ribbons bounce all over their heads as they rolled around in their own laughter, rocked with it, waiting for the wave of it to rise and then diving into it just as it crested, letting it break over them and pummel them to the ground, jumping up again with fresh gales, fresh hurricanes of laughter. Karen would stand in the kitchen doorway, hands on aproned hips, virtuously quelling the impatience in her voice as she tried for the fifteenth time to call the three of you to dinner.

Yes Frankie was as he put it royally pissed off at his daughters' affection for you and indeed at everyone else's too — as far as he was concerned it was nothing but unhealthy indulgence and could only serve to encourage your indecisiveness and self-pity. According to him what you really needed was someone to tell you the unvarnished truth about yourself rather than joining you in your delusions of fallen grandeur. When for example you confessed in a letter to Ruthie, quite humorously of course, that Michael's presence had prevented you from writing so much as a line for several years, she was overwhelmed with sorrow and remorse — but when she tearfully explained this to her brother over the phone, Frankie responded with a snicker and a snarl. Give up, Ruthie, he said, why don't you just give up? When are you finally going to face it? The old man never has amounted to anything and he never will, he'll always pick up the first monkey wrench that comes to hand and toss it into his own works so that he can go on moaning about the external factors responsible for his impotence, first this went wrong then that went wrong, but all his problems are of his own making — like the ghost stories he used to tell us when we were kids — he conjures them up on purpose so that he can stand there quaking, paralyzed with fear. His paralysis is not your fault, Ruthie, never believe that, it's not anybody's fault, it's a self-inflicted wound but he acts as if it were a glorious war injury — he's proud of it! He'll never relinquish it! So stop feeling sorry for him — that's just what he wants, can't you see? That's what makes his little theatre go on functioning year after year!

Ruthie was chilled to the bone by cruelty. It took her by surprise every single time, she could not get used to it and she did not know what to do with it. So rather than countering Frankie's arguments with other arguments she decided to keep her hurting for you to herself from that day on. Only later, much later, would she share a little of it with me.

Because yes, this is where I come into the story, feetfirst through the used and abused vaginal canal of that warm-hearted daughter of yours: Paula, her second bastard, named after a French-Canadian poker-player whose name was Paul. That was about all I ever learned about my old man since he skipped town as soon as the news of my as-yet imperceptible existence reached his ears. Fortunately, Ruthie did not even consider having an abortion this time — she was working in a gallery on Yorkville, earning decent money and able not only to take Michael back but to make a place for me.

You gave up Michael with a horrendous wrenching of the heart that made you breathless for weeks, then slowly eased off into a permanent chest cramp. He was going on six years old and you had attended his growth as you never had the growth of your own children, seen him leave behind the white cotton diapers with their giant safety pins which you called danger pins and move on to the potty then the toilet, soothed his fevers with a washcloth dipped into a basin of cool water and gently laid across his forehead, again and again throughout the night, taught him silly piano duets like *Chopsticks* and *In the Mood*, watched him explore the garden on his grubby hands and knees, pointed out to him the light green of the new caragana leaves in spring and the way they got darker and stickier as summer wore on, shown him how to suck the sweet yellow crescents of the caragana flowers, plastered mud on his beestings, barbecued steaks for him on the back porch despite Karen's acute distaste for the messiness of outdoor cooking, read him countless bedtime stories from good old *Treasure Island* to good new Doctor Seuss, to say nothing of the unsurpassable *Winnie the Pooh*, and the two of you had laughed until your stomachs hurt at the cowardice of Piglet and the gluttony of Pooh and especially oh especially the self-pitying sighs of Eeyore, and he had trusted you and *Grandpa* had become the warmest word in the English language and you had fixed in your memory the image of his smooth little hand abandoned in your worn and callused palm as he slept in your lap on the bus coming home from the planetarium, and although Karen saw to the feeding and cleaning of Michael's body with her usual conscientiousness it was you he worshipped, you he considered his companion in the universe, you his pal the rough gruff bear that took him hiking in the foothills and then spun yarns as long and shining as Rapunzel's golden hair so he would not get cranky on the way back.

Ruthie his mother had called and written constantly over the years though she was rarely able to afford the trip out West; to Michael she had seemed as splendid and inaccessible as the women on TV who fell in love with Zorro or Wyatt Earp, but always it had been understood that one day she would take him back, and then gradually it became feasible, and then abruptly it became real, and both of you Michael and you Paddon cried at the train station but Michael was six and you were sixty, Michael could go on to better things and you could not, and for the first time you wondered whether there was actually anything more important in life than being with the people you loved, whether time was of any interest whatsoever when clearly the salient feature here, clearly the invasive aggressive derisive divisive factor here was space: the preposterous number of miles that separated Calgary from Toronto. What kind of a world is this anyway, you asked yourself, in which little boys can be nonchalantly plucked from their grandfathers' arms, tossed into a train and spirited away in a puff of smoke?

For the first couple of years Michael wrote to you once a month as promised, stilted polite letters which to him were a burden and to you a frustration, and then one day his father turned up out of the blue, he had seen Ruthie's name on the gallery window and decided to surprise her, it was she who surprised him by informing him of the fifty-pound hockey-playing result of their drunken embrace of eight years earlier, and as she had nothing else to offer Michael in the way of a father, and as the father in question though balding and paunchy seemed to have acquired in responsibility what he had lost in physical attractiveness, the long and short of it was that from then on

Michael spent every school vacation down in Kingston where his father owned a house on the lake, discovered a hereditary passion for manly outdoor activities such as hunting and fishing, and forgot rather totally about you.

———— • • ————

John Sterling's men were getting fed up with his bad humour and bad luck, drifting away one after the other, leaving the ranch to run down and the horses to run wild, so that when after the hottest July in history England declared war on Germany your father fairly leaped to the nearest recruiting station to enlist.

Elizabeth was thrilled to pieces because she thought he was off to fight the Indians, she had heard about German atrocities at school and the only time that word had ever been used before was in connection with the Indians so she was proud of her daddy marching off to conquer this new tribe of savages and win them over to Christ's love. *Soldiers of the Cross arise! Gird you with your armour bright Mighty are your enemies Hard the battle ye must fight!*

As it turned out Canada was not quite ready for a war and there were not nearly enough uniforms to clothe all the fine sturdy ready young male bodies that turned up to join Calgary's Thirty-first Battalion, so your father donned his old South African slouch hat and riding breeches for the nonce. His hair was cut short leaving a white band of skin above the rest of his neck burnished red by the August sun and oh Paddon you could hardly recognize him and he kept joking about how he was going to visit the home country all expenses paid by the King and Wot yer pullin' that bleedin' face for, Mildred, don't yer know this is a stroke of luck for us and if I don't come back yer'll

176

get a lovely pension now, won't yer and the very next day you accompanied him to the train station — I can see that tiny Anton station with its mud and wooden planks and noise — you were still very small Paddon for your age you only came up to his shoulder and you kept looking down because the strangeness of his head and face disturbed you so that what you fixed in your mind at the moment of his departure were his shiny black boots and when he returned two years later you had grown to your full height which was taller than his but again you lowered your eyes when you saw him standing in the doorway, this time because your gaze was drawn to the lower part of his body by an absence and you saw that one of his pants' legs was pinned up at the knee and there was only one boot.

They're jolly and brave But never do rave About their pride and bravery Right at the front they stay In thickest of fray . . . They'll win the fight Their hearts are right You bet they're filled with pluck Right on their track When they come back We'll cheer our Johnny Canuck! — No one cheered. There must have been crutches and someone must have driven him to the house with his suitcase but I can't see any of that, I can just see you staring at him Paddon and you are so tall and gangly and he had not written or telegraphed once in the two years of his absence so you thought he was dead and he thought you were a little boy and the two of you had no idea what to do with each other and you did not exchange a single word. He hitched himself across the threshold into a house he had never seen before, let himself slump into the old armchair in one corner of the living room and undid the pin in his pants' leg. There was no thigh either, in place of the thigh there was a half-gallon bottle of contraband rye which he withdrew and, after

177

a second's hesitation, proffered you with outstretched arm in recognition of your pole-vault into manhood but you shook your head automatically, and when you realized you should have accepted it was too late and he was taking an angry swig by himself and had dismissed his patsy of a son once and for all.

It took him another nine years to drink himself to death. Not once did he mention the god-awful battle of Courcelette in which his left leg had been torn out at the root. Not once did he describe for your benefit or edification the trenches the corpses the mud and blood and shattered scattered limbs, the hopeless dark confusion of that war. Not once did he ask the slightest question about what had transpired back home in the meantime, if the word *home* could be used to cover such radically different situations as the one from which he had departed and the one to which he had returned.

The answer Mildred and Elizabeth did not volunteer to his unasked questions could be summarized in a single word, a one-syllable but flowing liquid silky smooth black word, the word oil, the beautiful gushing word *oil*, the word that meant rich, filthy rich, sticky gooey dark disgusting rich — yes, right on the property. Not that the Sterling women got any oil money directly, of course — they were not even aware that five hundred oil companies had splurted into existence in the spring of 1914 when Dingman No. 1 started ejaculating pure gorgeous burnable naphtha, they had not been witnesses to the scene on First Street Southwest that day in May when crowds of frenetic white men in suits and bowler hats trampled each other in the stampede to buy up shares, they had not watched the Calgary brokers gleefully filling their drawers with money until they overflowed, then stuffing the hundred-dollar bills and cheques into wastebaskets, indeed they knew nothing about shares and it was a good thing too because by the end of '14 most of the certificates for which Calgarians had shelled out a million dollars were being used as wallpaper but by that time the Sterling women had already pocketed a nifty price for the ranch.

They had been bracing themselves for a winter of nothing but pancakes fried in lard when the prospectors from Calgary Petroleum Products came by and announced their intention to begin drilling in the area, and before Mildred knew it a contract was being spread out right there on her oilcloth-covered kitchen table and she was being asked to sign something for the first time in her life. Of course it was her husband's signature she had to forge but the prospectors made it clear they trusted her and she was proud as hell to be taking such an important decision all by herself, the ranch had been declining anyway she reasoned and with the money she would be able to buy herself a house in town and perhaps even learn to drive a car and you Paddon could take piano lessons and Elizabeth would be safe from the leering sneers of the cowboys and besides, deep in her heart Mildred had always dreamed of moving back to the city and leading a proper existence again, full of tea with cream and crumpets and moral conversation, escaping the vast lost expanses of the ranch with its endless wind and wind and wind, its dismal ruts and furrows, its grey and dun monotony broken only by barbed-wire fences, and the nearest church forty-five minutes' walk away.

So much had changed! Mildred and Elizabeth had knitted and yakked their way through those two years in Calgary. They had gotten together with other women ostensibly to knit wash-cloths and bandages and socks and belly-bands for the men at the front but in fact they spent their time yak-yak-yakkety-yakking even faster than they knitted so that by the time John Sterling and the other servicemen made it back to Alberta not only had all the Big Valley brothels been burned down but women had wangled themselves the right to vote and promptly voted in Prohibition, making it impossible for an honest man to buy an honest drink!

Nothing remained of the old life. The ranch had been sold by the females lock stock and barrel, John could not have mounted a horse again even if there had been a ranch, his son instead of taking over as the man of the house sat at the piano playing drivelly music written by sissies with powdered wigs, his daughter ran around talking out loud to the bleedin' Virgin Mary, and his wife divided her time between crab-apple pre-serves and Temperance meetings. John Sterling stewed in a bit-ter silence. Mildred saw to it that the sheets on the living-room sofa were changed once a week; otherwise she paid him no attention whatsoever.

Temperance meetings were sometimes held at the house in which case your help would be enlisted, first to hide your father on the second floor — he leaned heavily on your shoulder and grumbled and groaned as he hopped from step to step and it tor-tured you Paddon to feel his skinny knobby body bumping up against yours in the narrow staircase — then to make conversa-tion with the newly arrived ladies as your mother and Elizabeth prepared the tea-tray. You would squirm as these God-fearing suffragettes pried distractedly into your heart with questions such as What's your favourite subject at school dear or Are you still taking piano lessons, to which you longed to respond by spitting or farting or slamming the door in their faces — thus began I would imagine your lifelong allergy to small talk, ah this was wonderful about you Paddon, this stubborn refusal to swap banalities or relinquish any information about yourself to people who meant well but meant nothing and whose aggressive gregariousness was to become increasingly popular with every passing decade thanks to the let-it-all-hang-out generation and then the I'm-OK-you're-OK generation — invariably you would dig in your heels and cut short the sort of conversation that began innocently with Nice day, isn't it? as if to generate a minimal warmth between members of the same species, then rapidly moved on to intolerably intimate questions such as Where are you from or Are you married or What line of work are you in, which though pronounced with an identical air of innocence set your teeth on edge, implying as they did that what you did was who you were or, worse, what you wanted to be doing.

The only time John Sterling ever emerged from his despondency again — and by this time you had left home and were trying to put him as far from your thoughts as possible — was when in 1919 Prince Edward discovered a taste for busting broncs and the province of Saskatchewan organized a giant rodeo in honour of His Royal Highness. Determined to have the pleasure of watching him break his royal arse, your father demanded that Mildred drive him, in the brand new Ford which she manoeuvred as brutally as your soul, all the way to Saskatoon. To his mortification however, as your mother told you over the telephone, the prince rode like a pro and the twenty thousand spectators fairly fainted away with ecstasy. The following month Prince Edward bought up the famous EP ranch a mere stone's throw away from the old Sterling property, and your father relapsed forever into drunken despair.

———————

In June, Calgary welcomed with open arms the relief-camp trekkers from B.C. — young single angered men in rags, fed up with being kept out of sight out of mind and doing useless back-breaking work for room and board and two insulting pennies a day, thousands of them clambering onto freight-train boxcars and advancing towards Ottawa like a menacing cloud of hoppers. But the hoppers would be stopped short in Regina a few days later and, a policeman having been killed in the confusion, train-hopping would be declared a federal crime. Namby-pamby Prime Minister Bennett was trembling in his expensive leather shoes. He waved his arms threateningly, gave orders for the Communist party leaders to be arrested and their literature seized and asked his dear law-abiding citizens to denounce each other for cheating on the dole.

Alberta meanwhile was leaning farther and farther to the right despite a few agitating or at least agitated farm workers who insisted that with such incredible resources and such huge amounts of work to be done it was grotesque to be kicking foreigners out of the province because of unemployment. But foreigners were in the process of becoming filthy Red rabble and William Aberhart now started slipping larger and larger dollops of Major Douglas's Social Credit theory, though he didn't understand it any too clearly, into his radio gospel sermons. The economic movement from God

Himself! he proclaimed and three hundred thousand listeners sat up and took note. Oh Lord grant us a foretaste of Thy millenial reign! Organization is not enough, our help must come from above! he thundered and they cheered and spread the word. Douglas in one hand, the Holy Ghost in the other! he roared at one evangelical picnic after another and they applauded until their hands burned crimson. If you elect me I shall give you prosperity certificates! he promised — but if you have not suffered enough, it is your God-given right to suffer some more! They elected him by a landslide, replaced R.B. Bennett with Mackenzie King, took their funny money to the empty stores and suffered some more.

You Paddon spent hours reading the newspapers. You did not even pretend to be working anymore, you just read the newspapers from start to finish and sometimes from finish to start. Once, just once, you the historian made a herculean effort to think about what was happening, concentrating for an entire weekend on the horrors at hand and producing a single paltry paragraph which was somehow saved from the wastebasket:

> North America is clearly converting its guilt for the extermination of the redskins into an exorbitant and unreasoning terror of the Reds — as though the Communists were neither more nor less than the ghostly reincarnation of the murdered Indians, come to take revenge, come to despoil us of the land we stole and desecrated . . .

You could go no further. Karen kissed you on the forehead when you emerged from your brown study and timidly asked Why don't you go down and march in the United Married Men's Parade? Oh Jesus, you answered, slamming the door.

There was nothing you could do.

On bad days you wore your frustration like an icy coat of armour which covered you from head to foot, making everything sharp and clear-cut and faraway, forcing you to move with extreme slowness and yearn for sleep. Many days were not bad though, so long as you kept away from the ancient questions furiously banging their fists against the locked door inside your head and turned your attention to what was happening around you. You accompanied Ruthie and Frankie to the Stampede for example and took delight in their delight when the Mickey Mouse float went by, laughed at their squeals and peals of laughter as the impeccably uniformed gold-braided marching trumpeters clarinettists trombonists and drummers strived to reach a compromise between stepping rigid and regular straight ahead and avoiding the steaming reeking plops of dung that lay in the path of their shiny leather shoes. Horses were everywhere — you sneezed your way through the entire day and made a joke of it. They were impressed to learn that you had attended the first Stampede ever and would not have believed you had you told them it was atrocious so you told them it was wonderful. You enjoyed walking through the crowd with each of your hands clasping the hand of a child, a nine-year-old and a seven-year-old, a boy and a girl, eyes agoggle and hearts craving to be thrilled and thrilled again. You were glad you had decided to splurge. You squeezed their hands.

Yes there were good days or at least good moments, many good moments in fact, such as those Saturday mornings when both you and Karen slept in and were wakened by little bodies snuggling up between you or by little fingers tickling your feet

184

or sometimes even by the smell of coffee as Frankie and Ruthie proudly carried in a breakfast tray — this was only on Saturdays, it would have been a shameful luxury on Sundays when by eight o'clock Karen was already rustling and bustling to get the three children and herself dressed and combed and spiritually spruced-up for church, the two of you having reached a compromise on this issue whereby she was allowed to expose them to her beliefs as long as there was no praying in the house, thus you were permanently delivered of grace and had Sunday mornings to yourself as they traipsed out into the cold, taking turns pushing Johnny's baby buggy up and down the steep icy streets to the Lutheran church a mile away since Karen didn't drive.

All of this is vivid to me Paddon, all these snatches of happiness and more: telling jokes around the supper table, making up ghost stories on summer nights, tobogganing or bobsledding on winter afternoons, fooling around with all three kids on the living-room rug, letting them take turns diving into you as if you were a swimming-pool or wriggling to free themselves from your bear-hug grip although these tussles often ended up in tears, Johnny's tears, and your annoyance that he should still be acting like a baby at the ripe old age of three.

Johnny tended more and more to avoid you.

Ruthie idolized you, and though she lived in dread of your outbursts, was old enough by the time she reached seven to consider them childish and forgive you for them — you would always blush to remember, for instance, how that same year 1935 you bought her a ten-cent toy watch so she would overlook your coming late to pick her up at the library, and after an initial crow of delight when you handed it to her on the streetcar she subsided into sulking because it was not the real watch she dreamed of owning so you saw red and, using unforgivably foul language to tell her what you thought of spoiled brats, snatched it from her hands and tossed it out the window as the streetcar clanged at top speed down Nineteenth Street. The scene could have grown very ugly at this point but Ruthie while shocked and hurt to the quick for herself was even more pained for you, ashamed at your having allowed her to see you acting so abominably, fearful you might gag on your guilt — and so, heroically overcoming her chagrin, she changed the subject.

As for Frankie — from what I can gather these were the last months of any kind of warmth between you and Frankie — he thought you were terrific. You were a schoolteacher! He looked up to you, boasted about you, brought home scintillating report cards to make you proud, loved it when you pummelled him and wrestled with him and treated him like a man. Karen was so relieved to see you taking an interest in life again that she dared not ask whether you had given up the idea of writing a book. So you learned to live from day to day, and to walk gingerly on the thin crust of normality which had formed over the festering sores of your hopes.

Under it all, under it all always, deep down, right next to the bone, was fear.

———◆———

Elizabeth came home on furlough that fall. Her hair was already streaked with grey but her blue eyes blazed more brightly than ever. Karen listened devoutly as her sister-in-law described the campaign recently launched in Haiti by the Catholic missions against the Monstrous Mixture. You listened not devoutly but with as much calm as you could muster; you had long ago discovered that it sufficed to register the tone of her voice and to murmur every now and then either Isn't that dreadful? or Isn't that nice? and she would be content with your conversation. There was a new isn't-that-nice tale involving a Haitian peasant named Ti-Jules, and as she told it tears came to Elizabeth's shining eyes and glittered in their light. Like all Haitian peasants Ti-Jules believed in voodoo, so when three of his children fell ill he went to the *houngan* and followed his instructions to the letter. But one day Our Saviour came and knocked at the door of his heart and he heard the knock at last and decided to let Him in. He rose from prayer and ran about the house smashing every object the *houngan* might have touched — chairs, plates, glasses, virtually all of his family's possessions. To his horrified wife he explained that he was getting rid of Satan's influence. Isn't that nice? you said.

Well, Elizabeth went on, God kept His part of the bargain and the children got better. Ti-Jules was so thankful he decided to share the Good News. He had a vision in which two Holy Fathers with glowing faces appeared to explain how he should go about teaching people to pray. His neighbours heard tell of the miracle and before long there were peasants travelling from far and wide to see him, all of them anxious to be free of their terrible voodoo spirits. Ti-Jules explained they had to get married if they were living in sin, promise never to touch a fetish again, burn down their mystery-houses and chop down their *arbres-servis*. You never know, admitted Elizabeth, which trees might be *arbres-servis* and which are just ordinary trees, but we generally feel it's better to cut down too many than too few. We've done a good bit of lumberjacking down there ourselves. Isn't that nice? you said. Of course, Elizabeth went on, her voice thrilling to the suspense, the voodoo priests and witch doctors were furious about losing their clientele. They denounced Ti-Jules to the authorities, accusing him of holding black magic ceremonies and being a political rabble-rouser. He was arrested and thrown in jail. Isn't that dreadful? you said. But Jesus stuck with him, so when he was released his reputation was bigger and better than ever! Literally thousands of peasants flocked to his home at Trou d'Eau. He's not ordained, of course, Elizabeth added, he doesn't really have the right to preach, all he can do is send them to their own parish priests and let them take over from there. Still, it's a great help to us to have one of their own people explaining things to them. Someone who knows voodoo from the inside. Isn't that dreadful? you said, having lost the drift of her argument but your sister was oblivious to any possible irony on your part — Ah, she concluded with a contented sigh, the hand of the Lord certainly does move in mysterious ways, doesn't it? And Karen sighed in echoing admiration.

For the next year there was not a single letter from Elizabeth that did not depict the spectacular progression of the *renonce*. Most of the peasants while making great outward shows of repentance still preferred to play it safe, taking Communion on the one hand and holding *manger-loa* on the other, placating the traditional powers while appeasing the new ones and hoping the sky wouldn't fall on their heads. Thus the priests had no choice, Elizabeth explained, but to punish them. They refused Communion to those who practised the Monstrous Mixture, inflicted six

188

months of penitence on anyone caught wearing an amulet, forbade drumming which was a means of calling up the *loas*, and exorcised putative werewolves — women accused of eating other people's children — by pressing New Testaments to their throbbing and curvaceous black chests and restraining them through hours of passionate writhing and panting until the evil spirit was at last expelled and the women collapsed, exhausted.

Despite all our efforts, said Elizabeth, those blacks kept returning to their heathen ways. They got sneakier and sneakier about it. They'd build shrines that looked exactly like Catholic altars, but when I'd come to visit a woman in labour, I'd see grains of corn scattered near one of the saints and a telltale bowl of water left next to the Virgin Mary. The family would hotly deny there was anything fishy going on, but all the mission doctors and nurses kept making the same discoveries. Finally we had no choice but to call on the government. Luckily, President Lescot is a good Catholic and has agreed to send the army to our assistance. These are crucial moments. Pray for our success. Will keep you posted. Love in Christ. Elizabeth.

And so it was that while the world's eyes were riveted on the mesmerizing moustache of Adolf Hitler, the voodoo temples of Haiti were systematically laid to waste. The University of Ottawa, which was run by Oblates, bestowed an *honoris causa* doctoral degree upon President Lescot in recognition of his courage. The whole thing made you tingle with rage and since you knew Karen was on Elizabeth's side the only person with whom you could share your rage was Miranda, who had many years before digested it and turned the greater part of it into laughter so as not to have her tender insides corroded by it.

Thus she responded with irony rather than indignation when you told her about the excited black and white priests striding from house to house and shack to shack and lean-to to lean-to, smashing peristyles and sacred dishes, burning family sanctuaries and confiscating every object that looked either remotely suspicious or remotely valuable, pocketing the latter and piling up the former in gigantic pyres that blazed all over the Haitian countryside to the glory of God.

Then in February '42, just as the preacher at Delmas church near Port-au-Prince was about to inaugurate a week of anti-superstitious sermons, someone opened fire on the congregation. This, for you, was the final straw. You decided you had to do something.

Oh I have come this far Paddon and suddenly for some reason I cannot go one word further, cannot hear or see or believe another thing about this life of yours I'm trying to invent. It's such a mysterious process — and wherever I leave off the picture seems to be complete, just as in Miranda's paintings there were never any empty spaces — I sit here at my desk in Montreal day after day and close my eyes and strain to hear and then a voice bubbles up and slowly starts to flow across the plain, across the page, and at times its song is wistful and at other times it's full of joy, telling me Miranda, telling me three children, telling me even about myself and my French-Canadian father Paul — oh Paddon I can't exist without you, don't take these words from me, I'm not trying to do you any harm . . . We need each other, Paddon.

No. It's no use. Nothing, not a sound. This frightens me horribly. I get up from my desk, go downstairs and take a long slow walk around the block. The city glitters neon all around me, French voices laugh together over foaming glasses of beer at the Expresso Café; I think of Crowfoot's visit, recall the look on his face when he posed to have his picture taken here in Montreal, the tension around his mouth, the defeat in his eyes, the shock of discovering white people living layered on top of each other all the way to the sky, streaming in and out of buildings, driving up and down paved streets (a sentence comes back to me, intact after two decades of cold storage in that part of my brain reserved for useless statistical information: Canada's Indians do not pose nearly as great a problem as America's Blacks because they represent only one as compared to ten per cent of the population — I repeat it under my breath for several minutes, one rather than ten per cent of the population, pronouncing the words with the inane precision of a cash register), then I recall the photos of the Blackfoot kids standing next to their desks at the mission schools, looking absolutely bewildered and lost, so uncomfortable in their starched tan uniforms, and I can feel my heart breaking again as it does each and every time I see these photographs, but then I think what does it matter, why do I keep returning to those people of a hundred years ago, why don't I just look around me, my contemporaries have their own bewilderments and losses, right here right now this very summer only twenty miles away from Montreal the Mohawks are staging a revolt, building barricades and blocking bridges and making headlines with their masks and machine-guns and American mercenaries, finally after all these years saying no to the Whites, no you cannot turn your nine-hole golf course into an eighteen-hole golf course by nibbling away yet another corner of our miserable shrinking plot, as a matter of fact this whole fucking area is our property including the city of Montreal itself and this time there's no two-timing treaty you can whisk out of your back pockets to prove differently . . .

Ah but somehow the dead are more alive to me than the living, which may be why your voice Paddon began to sing in me so powerfully when you died, only now it has stopped. These past few days, strain as I might, I can hear nothing at all.

Why won't you sing to me anymore?

All right. I know. I'm the one who's doing the singing. And I haven't yet told the truth about the reason why. And I'm afraid because I can feel the end of the song approaching and before it comes I'll have to find a way to tell that truth. For the moment I'm still not quite ready, I still need to string a few more beads onto this magic necklace of lies. For example I'd like to say a little more about my uncle Johnny, the youngest and most vulnerable of your kids. I've been avoiding him for a long time, I'm not sure why. For a while I thought he must have committed suicide, but now I think no, he's probably still around. (Nobody's gonna die in this story — I mean except everybody, as Miranda would say — this ain't the United States!) He can't have killed himself because I don't want there to be any real asperities in your existence Paddon, I want you to have led a plain ordinary life and been worthy of a gigantic love like Miranda's. Or like mine. Admittedly a character like Miranda is exceptional not to say far-fetched but she exists, there's no doubt in my mind about that and I hope there's none in yours either. Johnny exists too but for the moment he's still blurry — not much more than a shape, a series of adjectives.

Please, Paddon. Just a little while longer. Tell me how it was.

———————•◦•———————

Johnny was still out in B.C., he was in his early forties by this time and he'd never settled down, just drifted from one job and one town and one crash-pad to another until he wound up on the coast, Vancouver Island, he even tried California for a while but was immediately sniffed out by the American military in hopes he might be draftable so he drifted back up to Victoria and started buying and selling drugs, he loved the drizzle and the mildness of West Coast weather which allowed him to wander as he wished at any time of the day or year, hitchhike up the coast and drop a hit of psilocybin and spend the night alone on the shifting sand amidst grey driftwood sculpted by the sea, and it was a good thing fashion was dictating torn blue jeans and long hair because that was Johnny's permanent accoutrement. He had dreamy dazed blue eyes and the sweetest smile in the world and a ponytail, he spoke so softly you could hardly hear his voice and I think that must have been because of your shouting Paddon, and come to think of it I'm almost certain he was a lover of men, yes I can see a tattered copy of Kerouac in his knapsack, I imagine him smoking a few reefers and feeling his head begin to swirl, kissing the smiling men who happened to be in the park with him and following them to their homes and getting laid and being glad of their caresses but also glad of a bed and a shower and breakfast afterwards, perhaps he got arrested once or twice and the truth came out — Elizabeth must have been relieved to find a new subject for her prayers, a fresh batch of sins to fantasize about in hair-raising detail . . . I can see him now, yes, clean and calm and cool, very cool, no he most certainly did not commit suicide but you had nothing to say to each other Paddon, and Johnny never wrote. You tried to understand his endless wandering there on the far side of the Rocky Mountains, the reason behind his smiling and smoking and swirling, hollow as driftwood, forever on the surface of things, and you realized one day:

> *This is the crowning irony: my children destroyed my book and my book destroyed my children.*

Yes darling Paddon you now knew it was too late, you were getting old and tired, your hair was greyer and sparser than it had once been and your body heavier of course but you were teaching still, teaching still, unplugging your car at seven in the morning on the murderously cold black winter days, letting it warm up for fifteen minutes as you shovelled the walk, brushed heaps of snow from the hood and scraped the frosted windows back to something like transparency, then driving across the city as the bleak dawn broke, up hills so steep it could take fifteen tries for your momentum to overcome the slush, down hills so treacherous you could lose control of the wheel and spin wildly across patches of ice through three-hundred and sixty degrees and more, reaching the high school at long last (it had tripled in size since you were first hired there), parking your car and walking down the dim brown corridor to the teachers' room, glancing at the newspaper as you unbuttoned your overcoat and the minute-hand jumped its way to nine o'clock, then heading for the classroom, wearily bowing your head as the Lord's Prayer and *O Canada*, now prerecorded, were piped in over the loudspeaker, then proceeding to explain to the grandchildren of your first students that Samuel de Champlain had died on Christmas Day 1635 and that the French troops led by General Montcalm had lost the Battle of the Plains of Abraham to the British troops led by General Wolfe, then passing out multiple-choice exams to make sure everyone had gotten it straight. You stood there five days a week in your suit and tie, wearing a white shirt impeccably ironed and starched by your perfect wife, and you taught your heart out.

Elizabeth retired in '63 and it was about time too because Duvalier needed more elbow-room and was kicking out foreign priests and missionaries left and right, her hair was snow-white but her body still as powerful as ever and her pristine soul unsullied by thirty-six years of pouring medicine and gospel into savages. Haiti in the meantime had gone from very bad to very much worse, its forests had been chopped down and used as fuel so its topsoil had washed away into the sea and its peasants, poor in the thirties, were starving in the sixties, and a Haitian egg fertilized by a Haitian spermatozoid had a less than even chance of celebrating its first birthday on the face of the dusty dead eroded Haitian earth but a better than even chance, thanks to the efforts of the Church, of being baptized before returning to its Maker. Your sister now left the parched and wilted white-raped black republic in the hands of that same Maker, waving goodbye for the last time to the enormous pink-and-yellow cathedral that overlooked the bay, there were airplanes by this time of course to bring her from Port-au-Prince to Calgary, and at every stopover Miami New York Toronto she saw newspaper-vendors rushing about and women weeping and fainting and babies wailing and men frowning as hard as they could to hide the fact that they were almost weeping too because a very historic bullet had just entered the brain of a very historic man and the brain and the bullet were still vying to see which of them would get the upper hand but by the time the wheels of Elizabeth's airplane touched down on the runway at Calgary International it was the bullet.

She was glad to be home for good. Calgary had been more and more difficult to recognize each time she had returned on furlough. It had never stopped sprouting new houses and schools and oil derricks and churches and skyscrapers, proliferating in all directions including up and down and rejoicing in itself, boasting that as far as surface area went it was now the largest city in the dominion, laughing superciliously at Edmonton which had just launched an annual celebration called Klondike Days in memory of the gold rush that had lured your dad from London and done so much for the prosperity of the town, now kids got to pan for phoney nuggets and grown-ups got to fork out real dollars for gambling and hamburgers, but nothing could compete with the Calgary Stampede whose world-famous chuck-wagon racing was probably, as the tourist brochures Elizabeth brought home from the airport modestly allowed, the most thrilling sport known to man and whose visitors this year would be treated to an exciting portrayal of the Blood Piegan Stoney Sarcee and Blackfoot Indian cultures as the Stampede errupted [sic] in a kaliedescope [sic] of pageantry. You sighed as you glanced through these brochures filled with

196

shameless money worship and spelling mistakes, reflecting that brawn would forever win out over brain in these parts of the world and wondering if your fifteen years of loving a woman named Miranda formerly Falling Star formerly Shining Star had been a dream.

You retired in '65 and I too started coming out West each year for the month of July, and since my three-years-older cousins delighted in teasing and spooking and bossing me, since they had their own unbreakable code of communication and often seemed to form a single entity, unpredictable and intimidating, you Paddon took my side always, the games we played were Paddon and Paula against Pearl and Amber and when you accompanied us to the Stampede you always found some secret thing to share with only me. For us as kids the Stampede was not the parade, not the rodeo, not the white Stetsons and bucking broncs and Indian floats — all of which we found as hopelessly corny and old-fashioned as Westerns on TV — for us the Stampede was the fairgrounds. I started saving my pocket money right after Christmas and as of June my dreams were a voluptuous mixture of Ferris wheels and cotton candy and roller-coasters and candied apples — oh that was one sweet fast week you took us through Paddon, everything as disgustingly sweet and dangerously fast as possible, we wanted nothing more than to lose ourselves in the blatant voices and garish colours of the crowd and to ride on our own adrenaline until we dropped.

The only summer I missed was '67 because Ruthie decided it was more important to be out East that year to celebrate the hundreth anniversary of Confederation, so instead of staying with you I stayed with Pearl and Amber's cousins in Montreal, took the sophisticated French subway all the way to Ile Ste-Hélène and saw the Centennial Exposition and World's Fair, visiting pavilions and riding the mini-train and watching batons twirl and trumpets glitter and fireworks explode until my head swam. In the midst of all this excitement you sent Ruthie a dry little note pointing out that only recently the French had gotten kicked out of Algeria on their asses after having settled there a hundred years before, taken over the country and its government, claimed it as their own and built it in their image, and wondering if it might not be dangerous for Canadians to indulge in premature rejoicing about their victory over the natives of this land.

I remember that note because Ruthie was shaken as she read it, I watched her face turn from pink to white to grey and it was the only time she ever criticized you in front of me — Sometimes it really does seem, she said with a slight tight sigh, that he takes pleasure in spoiling other people's fun, bringing them down to his level of hopelessness and gloom.

But maybe you were just missing me Paddon, maybe what you were really bitter about was my absence?

Meanwhile in Toronto Frankie and Clorinde had turned their house into a welcome centre for draft dodgers as a constant stream of them was now flowing north across the border with middle-class white bodies they cared about keeping in one piece. Frankie telephoned every now and then to chat with his mother but he and Clorinde almost never came out West, their lives were fuller than ever what with the incredible demands on their time and energy, not just setting up job interviews for these poor American boys and pulling strings to get them residence permits in Canada but also attending anti-war demonstrations and preparing their own seminars and lectures and court cases and colloquia, to say nothing of helping Pearl and Amber through their adolescent crisis. If the truth be told — though this truth was carefully concealed from you by all of us — it was not Pearl and Amber who were in crisis but Frank and Clorinde because of Pearl and Amber, and it had nothing to do with adolescence but with a phenomenon which was considerably more enigmatic, not to say inexplicable, and therefore intolerable to their adamantly enlightened father: increasingly, the girls appeared to be endowed not only with the gift of mutual telepathy, relatively common in twins, but with other, less innocuous powers.

Now I wish you had known about this, Paddon, because I think it would have made you glad, I think you would have seen it somehow as a rebirth of Miranda, a tiny post-mortem victory of the medicine men she had revered — a proof that no matter how energetically it is attacked, mystery will never be overcome. Yes, though huddled much of the time in their poster-plastered bedroom trading Beatles bubble-gum cards, Pearl and Amber claimed responsibility for the catastrophic lack of rainfall in Quebec, the sudden cracking of their father's rearview mirror (Amber told him the exact minute at which it had occurred), and the violent stomach-aches accompanied by vomiting and diarrhea of no less than three draft dodgers who had come to the house to discuss their situation.

Clorinde did her best to scoff but she was visibly impressed and Frankie was outraged that she should slide back even half a step towards the superstitious murk of her Caribbean childhood. Clorinde had in fact been carrying her mother's words and warnings around with her all these years, she had never forgotten the triumphant smile on the old blind woman's face the first time she had taken the twins to visit her in Montreal or the way she had said Yes, the Marassa have returned, I knew they would, they've come all the way to Canada to find us, the Marassa have returned and the country's going to be all right, just be sure you train their power properly so it doesn't run wild, so they don't turn it against you or each other, never make them jealous, always give them exactly the same things. And the little girls had remained peaceful as the old woman took them in her arms and bathed them and massaged them gently with orange leaves and papaya leaves, then swaddled them like the Baby Jesus of Prague and sat down with them in her rocking chair, crooning to them in Creole exactly as if they were on the shady veranda of her home in Jérémy instead of the second floor of a tacky little house in North Montreal surrounded by mounds of snow, rocking them back and forth with her blind eyes closed and the brown Haitian hills dancing and glancing in the sun behind the brown lids — The Marassa have returned, be sure you don't rub them the wrong way, even while they're small they can bè dangerous, they're very sensitive and you must take care to keep them on your side.

While never quite admitting it to herself, Clorinde had always followed this advice — perhaps especially since her mother had died a short while afterwards — always flattered her daughters with identical praise, always served them identical portions of food and switched their plates when they weren't looking so that each would partake of the other's meal, always avoided feeding them leafy vegetables such as watercress or sorrel which might have made them lose their powers, always watched them closely to make sure they were full of contentment and complicity, so that now when the gift began to show she could not help feeling proud and confessing it to her husband. Naturally Frankie was furious and said What the fuck are the Marassa? and Clorinde explained that they were the children of Saint Nicholas and Saint Claire, beloved and highly honoured ancestor twins whose magic was so powerful it was visited not only upon all twins but even upon their younger siblings, and Frankie stormed Come off it, Clorinde, after fifteen years of living in a literate country I hope you're not going to start handing me that crap! and the next day it was his turn to grab his stomach and retch and groan and puke. He began to be wary of his own daughters and his very wariness unnerved him because he found it ideologically inadmissible so that after a few months of sleepless nights he finally confided in his sister, but Ruthie who was tolerance incarnate merely suggested he see a doctor who could prescribe something for his insomnia.

Then to take everyone's mind off the hideous stifling images of jungle and napalm in Vietnam the United States sent a man to the moon and we sat together that summer evening of 1969 and watched the fuzzy blurry floating bobbing flag-planters on TV, then went out to the porch and you sank into the rocking chair and drew me onto your lap and talked and talked and talked to me, I don't remember the words you said but I can still hear the music behind them, and as you held me in your lap I watched one tear trickle down each of your wrinkled cheeks and wondered which of them would win the race, they slipped and slid and slowed and almost stopped, now one was ahead and now the other — Oh but the sky, Paula! you said, to think the sky has been made empty now, as empty as the land!

And you did not stop there Paddon, you could not stop there, you went on to explain more things to me about emptiness and fullness, taking me wholly into your confidence now, forgetting that I was nine years old, remembering only how very fervently I loved you, just as Heidi loved her own misanthropic misunderstood grandfather in the Alps, and you rocked and wept and held me in your confidence, and the salty droplets rolled into the moving corners of your mouth as it confessed to me the abandoned thesis and the almost book then the maybe book then the never book, and I, my heart drum-beating with the indignation of a child who loves, swore to you that I would find a way to help. Just as Heidi promised her grandfather she would return one day to his cottage on the Alm, I vowed to do all that was in my power to pick up the torch to which you had set fire, carry to completion what you had begun, ensure that your *Time and Time Again* (as you called it then) on this earth would not be wasted. I'll never marry or have children, I declared, pure and ardent as Joan of Arc, I'll go to university, learn everything you once learned and turn your manuscript into a book to end all books. I'll call it — my eyes raked the stars in a desperate search for something to delight you — *My Grandfather's Clock*. At this the dripping corners of your eyes crinkled into laughter and you took my hand in your two hands and solemnly accepted the promise of a child.

That was when it happened between us Paddon, that was when you staked out your claim to my existence, I'll never forgive you for planting your flag in my heart like that, it was my fault too but you were the adult and it was up to you to refuse, if not immediately then on one of a thousand possible occasions later on but you never did, for the next twenty years my life revolved around that promise and you knew it, deep down you knew and never lifted a finger to relieve me of its awful weight, the terrible sense of betrayal that engulfed me every time I swerved an inch from the path my eyes had traced in the stars that night so long ago — and of course I betrayed you, over and over: even when I did what I had promised it was betrayal because I did it for the wrong reasons, going to university but studying journalism instead of philosophy, spurning marriage but only because my love of women was too strong, renouncing children because what really mattered to me was my career.

Only now, now that you're dead and gone, can I face the fact that your wisdom will never be my own. These pages, Paddon, are the fragments of my broken promise — and the closest I shall ever come to writing *My Grandfather's Clock*. You left me your words and I am stitching them into a patchwork quilt that will serve you as a shroud.

You Paddon had other things to worry about. You were in high school now, no longer the one-room school in Anton with its obstreperous wood stove but a real city high school made of bricks and filled with books. You had begun to read in earnest and felt the first quiverings of flight in your soul's wings. Every evening after washing-up you would play the piano to release your thoughts, then climb to your room and sit on your bed and watch them plunge and soar. Elizabeth was already planning to become a nurse and for her things were simple and straightforward, God had taken her by the hand and she would go where He led and do what He said, her world was peaceful because He had made it in His infinite wisdom and it could therefore only be good and she was serene in the knowledge that His will must be done which meant both that she must do it and that whatever happened would be His will since He was responsible for everything and nothing ever happened that He had not willed, so Elizabeth shied away from books that might take her mind through the leaps and loops that so exalted yours; the only thing she wished to learn in books apart from the life of Christ was the human body and the only human bodies she would ever approach and touch when they were naked were suffering bodies, sick and wounded purulent bleeding moaning agonizing bodies and to these she would minister, over these she would bend fully dressed, thanks to these she would win new hearts to the Lord.

You Paddon were so thrilled by your intelligence you had a hard time figuring out what bodies were for. You chewed your food absent-mindedly, indulged in sports as rarely as possible and masturbated with the help of photographs from last year's yearbook. None of these activities afforded you any pleasure, they merely had to be gotten through for your mind to remain clear and calm. One evening you stood in your bathrobe staring out the window at the northern lights and feeling your ideas throb within their giant glowing curves and upon turning back to bed you accidentally caught a glimpse of your naked legs, long and pasty pablum white and hairy, and the sight of them not only shocked but sickened you, so incompatible did it seem with the glorious whorls of the septentrional heavens.

The Spanish flu epidemic only reinforced your aversion for physicality. Returning servicemen brought it to Calgary just as the war was drawing to a close in Europe, so Armistice Day looked like carnival as thousands of carousers attempted to keep their germs to themselves by wearing masks but, in spite of this precaution or because of it, the germs spread like prairie fire and you coldly followed their progression in the newspaper, certain that you yourself would be immune. Schools and churches were soon shut down and turned into hospitals, Elizabeth was only sixteen but she took it into her head to go around nursing the neighbours and overriding Mildred's objections she did it full time until of course she too caught the disease and passed it on to your father. By that time half the city was groaning and squirming between infected sheets; thermometers under tongues shot up while those on windowsills shot down; the cathedral was full of Indians unable to make up their minds whether to die of the flu or freeze to death; doctors and nurses dropped dead in their snowboots leaving families to fend for themselves; children expired in their beds and feverish parents were too weak to do anything about it; adults died and their friends dragged their bodies out of their houses and threw them into snowbanks since the ground was frozen solid and it was impossible to dig graves. You Paddon listened to the delirious praying of your sister, her tirelessly reiterated promise to devote her life to Christ if He should save it now, *Nevertheless not as I will, but as Thou wilt*, and you told yourself the body was nothing but a germ whereas the mind was a snowflake, the body was rankling and rot whereas the mind was geometrical perfection, the body was chaos and proliferation whereas the mind was icy calculation and control. The corpses in the snowbanks seemed to you an excellent demonstration of mind's triumph over matter.

Then the girl next door came to live with you because both her parents had died, she had a sweet soft name like Sara or Mara and your mother made you share with her the living-room couch you were sleeping on because the whole upstairs was given over to the flu, she ordered the two of you to sleep back to back with your clothes on but as of the very first night you sensed Sara's or Mara's inaudible sobs through the mattress and turned to put a comforting arm across her back, and as of the second night you were licking the salt tears at her throat and whispering that you would take care of her, and as of the third night you were pressing your hardness very gently against her backbone and touching with your fingers the miracle of a girl's sex through cotton drawers, exploring what unexpectedly was not a smooth sameness as on statues but a soft series of rills and ripples that made you dizzy, and by the time the epidemic was over and Sara's or Mara's aunt from Lethbridge could safely come into the city and pick up her niece, you had quite completely changed your mind about your body. All that spring you felt yourself thawing, and by the time the snow finally melted and the months-old corpses began to stink, you had fully come to your senses.

> The snowflake, like the flower of flesh beneath my fingertips, is only beautiful because I am there to sense it. One has no more mind than the other. The snowflake will melt and the flesh will rot; both their existence and their inexistence depend on time; intelligence too is inseparable from its flowering in time and its espousal of phenomena. Therefore God cannot exist.

That, I have decided after poring over your writings countless times and in every possible order, was the first fragment of original thought you ever committed to paper. You learned it at age eighteen thanks to a woman, and again at age thirty-six thanks to a woman — but you kept forgetting it, didn't you Paddon?

In the final years, fifteen of them perhaps, you had given up. You kept plodding along — as though you of all people had been taken in by that ancient ploy to make time stop, forcing each day to be identical to the one before, going grimly through a very small number of motions such as sitting by the window reading the newspaper filling your pipe drawing smoke into your lungs and slowly expelling it . . . You never played the piano anymore. Finally, having as you put it stopped pretending you had anything better to do, you even allowed Karen's fox terrier to spend entire afternoons in your lap.

From the newspaper or the telephone or your wife you learned of changes in the outside world — lots of deaths, Karen's bridge partners and coffee-cake bakers, your older and then your younger colleagues, dropping into darkness one after the other, because of this, because of that, hearts giving out lungs collapsing brains flooding with blood hipbones snapping discs slipping and memories getting smeared into mud. Your own mind and body were surprisingly intact, if unrelievedly inert, and you sometimes marvelled at the lengths to which people went nowadays to avoid death, dieting and exercising and enduring costly surgery — a new law had even been passed requiring chuck-wagon racers to wear safety-helmets and safety-belts if they wished to participate in the Stampede! You, meanwhile, sat there. Waiting.

Nothing could relieve your taciturnity, not even the party we threw for your eightieth birthday at which you were surrounded by your loving wife your loyal sister your sons your daughter your daughter-in-law your son-outlaw (Ruthie's new boyfriend) your three granddaughters your one grandson, now the proud owner of a sports and aerobics supply store, and even your first great-grandson — because the previous year Michael had married Susie who worked at the Toronto branch of International Weight Watchers and the two of them had gone over their accounts and decided that their combined salaries and savings in the bank and stocks and bonds and life insurance made it possible for them to plan a small family so Susie had had her IUD removed and they had had intercourse on the twelfth day of her cycle and conceived a child whom three successive ultrasound tests had revealed to be normal so there he was, little Bob, named after Susie's father but part of your family just the same, your gigantic loving family — all of them gathered around the table to sing *For He's a Jolly Good Fellow*, yes it was jolly miserable you were Paddon, moved to tears but miserable just the same.

That party was also the only time in my life I saw what I would call magic with my own eyes, I don't think you realized what was going on and those who did were too thunderstruck to breathe a word. Frankie had been even more hostile than usual throughout the day, he'd kept his mouth clamped shut while we sang and his hands ostentatiously flattened on the table when applause broke out to hail the arrival of the cake, a many-tiered splendour that Karen had made from scratch and decorated with her own hands. The eighty candles seen through your tears must have appeared a single blaze of light and you blew and blew at them with your wheezy weakened breath and had to turn the cake around to get at the ones on the back and everyone but Frankie was clapping and cheering and teasing you about how many girlfriends you had and I noticed Frankie getting tenser and tenser, I've just now realized that he must have been on the verge of blurting out something about your girlfriends, something that would have not only cast a pall over the celebration but marred your marriage once and for all, I could see everything in him beginning to rise, his fury, his indignation, his blood pressure, a flush of red washed up his neck and then his whole body embraced the upward movement, he leapt to his feet and cleared his throat, yes he had decided to do it, yes he would destroy you at long last, yes you deserved it, standing there weeping and wheezing and making everyone feel sorry for your ridiculous incapacity to blow out the candles. He was looking back and forth from you to Karen and trembling with rage that no one should be expressing gratitude to his mother who had baked the cake and piled the layers carefully on top of one another in diminishing sizes and squeezed hundreds of rose shapes from plastic icing devices up and down its sides and written Happy Birthday, Paddon on the top. Without their realizing it, everyone's attention was gradually being drawn away from you and turned apprehensively towards your son. And then it happened.

Pearl and Amber who were seated on either side of me suddenly at the same split second and without so much as glancing at one another reached across my lap and grabbed each other's hands. Instantaneously I saw Frankie falter and then freeze. He could not budge. It was as if every ounce of willpower in his body had been chained, padlocked, strait-jacketed. Clorinde reached out and put a hand on her husband's arm and said What is it Frank? What's the matter? Karen gave a little yelp of fear and you Paddon looked about in confusion, your myopic teary bleary vision further obfuscated by candle smoke. On the far side of the table your eldest son was no more nor less than a statue, utterly rigid, leaning on his arms like pillars, his hands still flattened on the tablecloth and his jaw ajar to speak. Then — gently, ever so gently — the twins' hands parted and their father slumped to his seat, dazed and disoriented like one who has just emerged from anaesthesia.

I was jubilant — for once that day, Paddon, the twins were on our side, the side of deep secret against shallow fact, the side of glimmering contradiction against glassy certainty, the side of tremulous Crowfoot against triumphant Lacombe. I think Clorinde knew perfectly well what had happened for in the look she threw her daughters I could read a mixture of shock, disapprobation and excited pride. Frankie had lost his long-awaited chance to give you your come-uppance, and was so shaken that he most likely abandoned the idea once and for all.

It was a short time after this that he and Clorinde separated, then divorced; when the Duvalier regime finally bit the Haitian dust in '86 Clorinde returned to her home country taking Pearl and Amber with her, and I haven't seen my lovely dangerous cousins since then. Mother received a card from Clorinde a few months ago announcing that both of them had gotten married the same day, a fabulous wedding celebration had been held in their honour and madly generous offerings of food and drink had been heaped upon them in hopes they would deign to cure the sick and punish the *tontons-macoute* and release the rain that had somehow gotten tied up there in the clouds.

Naturally the minute she heard about this Elizabeth crossed herself and kissed her rosary and fell to her knees.

Your wife was less demonstrative than your sister but every bit as earnest in her faith. Indeed, as you Paddon gradually wilted and withered and folded up into your despair, Karen's Protestant piety thrived and flowered and required increasing amounts of room in which to grow. She too must have been desperate — to keep you with her, to keep you alive, to protect her own reasons for living . . . So she amassed a mind-boggling collection of church gazettes, YWCA brochures, daily reminders, religious almanacs, prayer-circle and missionary society literature, little framed poems containing recipes for pious behaviour, illustrated and non-illustrated editions of the New Testament, and countless paperback books with titles like *How to Have a Personal Relationship with Christ* or *Where Will You Go From Here?* which she left within arm's reach of every seat in the house including the toilet seat. She prayed more and more often and audibly, memorizing handy little *Thoughts of the Day* to murmur under her breath as she went about her housecleaning.

The house got cleaner and cleaner — you had funded the purchase of abrasive products and various scraping and scratching and sucking and polishing devices designed to eliminate dust and food and grease and hair and other telltale traces of non-spiritual existence from its every nook and cranny though in Calgary's modern homes there were neither nooks nor crannies,

211

nothing but smooth flat innocent surfaces which met one another at right angles and had nothing to declare — Karen even dusted the tops of doors.

I was unable to return to Alberta after your eightieth birthday, Paddon. That was the last time I saw you — forgive me. What had seemed to me curious rituals as a child became insufferable ordeals as I grew up: Karen's continual surveillance and advice about being ladylike (which meant keeping my thighs tightly pressed together every time I sat down) and economical (which meant scraping every drop of cake batter from the bowl into the cake pan so there was no raw pleasure left over to be licked), her interminable Sunday-dinner grace during which the gravy on her thin pink slices of electrically carved roast beef coagulated and grew cold; her pitiless moral dissection of neighbours and their children, ministers and their sermons, TV advertisements and their teeth-rotting hype . . . You, Paddon, under the onslaught of her verbal barrage, were neither responsive nor resentful but resigned. You contented yourself with nodding — or, if no feedback was required, listening. Yes, listening. You were no longer capable of that minimal touch of rudeness or freedom, inattention. You forced yourself to listen — as though this were your burden here on earth and you intended to bear it with infinitely renewed patience, repressing your own thoughts again and again in order to concur that yes, the idea of allowing women into the ministry *was* preposterous or that yes, the neighbours *had* been remiss about mowing their lawn this year. She was allergic to serious conversation — you had not only monopolized seriousness but compromised it forever in her eyes — so that whenever anyone seemed about to become passionate or intense, she would assassinate their emotion with a well-aimed bullet of received wisdom such as It takes all kinds to make a world or You never know how life is going to turn out, do you? — irrevocably reducing particular tragedies or comedies to general platitudes.

During my last visit I happened to pick up the mother-of-pearl brush-and-mirror set that lay on the dresser near my bed, and she rebuked me gently for having replaced them on the doily at a slightly different angle. I don't mind your handling my things, Paula, she explained in her longest-suffering tone of voice, but please try not to make more work for me. That afternoon I waited for the two of you to go grocery shopping and then — in hopes of coming across some sign of *you*, Paddon, some minute hint of disorder or despair — rifled through every drawer in the house. But no. Nothing. All I found was well-laundered underwear, rows of empty lavender-water bottles and cold-cream jars, black and brown and navy blue socks and gloves rolled into pairs, immaculate linen in perfectly folded piles, more religious tracts and more New Testaments . . . I didn't think of looking in the attic. Perhaps by that time even you had forgotten your manuscript was decomposing up there.

———— • ————

Oh Paddon I had the most atrocious dream last night. I was on a city street somewhere — not physically present; I could see and hear but I couldn't intervene — there was a series of gunshots over to my left and, turning my gaze in that direction, I saw a crowd of people in an uproar. I asked Is anyone hurt? and the question itself provoked the instantaneous dispersal of the crowd and the appearance of a crumpled body on the ground. It was a woman. Is she dead? I asked, coming closer — and, because I had asked, she was dead. I moved still closer, unable to restrain my curiosity and put an end to the scene. Invisible hands lifted the woman so that I could inspect her wounds, and when they turned the corpse towards me I saw to my horror that it was Miranda. She was nude and larger than life, there was no blood on her body, she was returning to the earth and seemed to be made of clay. It's the Golem, I said to myself. Now my gaze began to search her body for wounds and everywhere it fell a wound appeared because it had fallen there. It fell on her eyes, they were gouged out. It fell on her chest, a deep hole was carved into the flesh above one breast. Aghast, I turned away before my gaze could attack and destroy the rest of her.

The dream appalled me because it suggested that what I'm doing here is just the opposite of what I had hoped to do — not stitching a shroud but defiling cadavers. Oh Paddon, I beg you — release me from my promise. Allow me to sing you to eternal sleep.

———————

Yes Paddon for once in your life you had to do something, not just think about doing something and wonder about doing something and regret and wish and yearn and hope and go around in circles from anger to self-control to forced indifference — you had come of age for the First World War just as it was ending and by the time the Second broke out you'd had too many kids to be drafted so never had you stood up and fought, never even as a child, not even defending yourself when those boys grabbed your toque away from you and started playing pig-in-the-middle, never learned to bust a bronc, never managed to make an imprint, an impact, decide on something and go through with it from beginning to end, so now by God you were going to do something, Paddon, and the only question was what.

If you had any influence anywhere, it was in your classes at school. You obviously couldn't teach a class on the scandal of the Haitian *rejetés*, but you could tell those kids — for once tell them the truth — that the same thing had happened right here in southern Alberta. That was it! You felt relieved when you came to this conclusion and realized it was exactly what you wanted to do, what you needed to do, and what for once in your life you were going to do.

You decided to concentrate on the figure of Father Lacombe. This instantly made you both excited and a little queasy, as though you were about to touch something taboo, defile some sacred object that might turn its forces against you. No historical personage was more revered by Elizabeth or more hallowed by your own high school instruction than the wandering Oblate with his silvery curls, his gentle face and his big black hat. Even your father, once long ago, had grudgingly acknowledged his greatness. Too bad, you told yourself as you rubbed your mental hands together, that's just too bad. It is time the truth were out.

All that spring you read up on the subject, taking notes and talking it over with Miranda until you were bursting with impatience to see how your students would react — would they blush with retrospective shame? Petition the government? Accuse their parents?

Apart from this one day, Paddon, I can see almost nothing of

215

your life at school. You never talked about it, never brought a colleague home for dinner, never shared with Karen the rare insight you came across in one of your students' papers, held it all inside you always. But this day I can see: a shimmering shiny day at the beginning of June 1942.

You gave the surprise lecture to each of your classes in turn, modifying the vocabulary according to the age of your students, feeling Miranda's strength surge through you all day long as you spoke, her strength and her pain, her pain and the dismay of the Haitian peasants, their dismay and the helpless indignation of the Moors attacked by the Crusaders, their indignation and the screams of the Spaniards burned at the stake by the Inquisition, their screams and the sobs of Jewish women raped in the bloody Prague pogrom of 1386, their sobs and the wail of Montezuma confronted by Hernán Cortés echoed in your ears, coursed through your veins, pounded in your chest Paddon as you recounted, with all the solemnity of which you were capable that day, the story of Father Lacombe.

How he had come here with the sole and firm and unswervable intention of changing what the Indians believed into what he believed. How he was prepared to put all of his skills and wiles at the service of this intention. How he had learned the Indians' languages only to force them to say things they had never intended to say. How he had taken advantage of their gullibility and superstition, their fascination with images and likenesses, to teach them the Christian version of history on long illustrated ladders climbing from the Creation of the universe to the Apocalypse and divided neatly into two with Good on the left and Evil on the right, depicting century after century of battles between the two, Luther and Mahomet and Arius trying to drag people over to the right-hand path which leads to hell, while hosts of missionaries and angels desperately attempted to pull them back to the heavenbound left.

How the Indians had been strong and healthy until the white man came and had then received from him the gift of civilization in the form of smallpox and measles and TB and scarlet fever and influenza, and how Father Lacombe and others of his ilk had made use of their vulnerability to convert them, giving them medical care in an ostentatious display of altruism, while telling them that those who died went to hell whereas those who recovered by the mercy of Christ were being given a last chance at salvation so they had better convert.

How Albert Lacombe had encouraged the Indians to sign Treaties No. 6 and No. 7, knowing full well that the Whites were lying through their teeth and that in any case provisions were always made in revoltingly abstract legal jargon which enabled Her Majesty to take back whatever land was being left to Her Indians whenever She bloody well felt like it.

How Lacombe had sat there and watched the Blackfoot starve to death since the government, surmising that they would only learn how to farm if they had to, was sending them five dollars per person per month instead of the twelve promised in the treaty, sending them — now that buffalo hides were inexistent — cotton sacks with which to make their tents, sending them bacon instead of beef, sending them less flour, less and less flour, even less flour this year than the year before, until the adults started eating gophers and mice, and then dogs and horses, and then the carcasses of animals they found rotting on the prairie, while the children writhed on the ground after swallowing poisonous wild parsnip.

How when, unable to bear the sight of their families dwindling and dying, Blackfoot students began deserting the Catholic Industrial School at High River in 1885, Father Lacombe told the government to threaten uncooperative parents with loss of rations. Better to have no food at all and believe in Christ our Saviour than to have a bellyful of buffalo beef and no sense of shame.

How when, after all the promises and breaking of promises and negotiation of new promises, the CPR had drawn its line right smack across the Blackfoot reserve and sent thousands of timber-cutters and rock-men clambering all over their mountains, it was once again Father Lacombe who had shown up, laden with bribes in the form of sugar and flour and tea and tobacco, to lie calmly and smilingly to the seven hundred armed braves that had gathered to prevent the driving of the stakes and the laying of the tracks.

Your voice trembled with emotion Paddon as you read aloud this final lie: Well, my friends — ah in that phrase you could hear the minister at Anton Methodist, you could hear Bible Bill Aberhart, you could hear Elizabeth in Haiti and every sly Jesus-mongering hypocrite in history — Well, my friends, I have some advice to give you today. Let the white people pass through your lands and let them build their roads. They are not here to rob you of your lands.

That day, a Friday, the response of your students was unfathomable but you went home happy with yourself and slept through the better part of the weekend. By Monday morning, the principal's office was swamped with complaints from irate parents — deviation from the curriculum — supposed to be preparing students for final exams — undermining Canadian patriotism just when it is most sorely needed— reeks of communism — blasphemy — a spiteful calumny of one of the most outstanding figures in the history of the West — a scandal. One venomous father even accused you of being in cahoots with the Japanese down around Lethbridge (stupidly imported from B.C. after Pearl Harbour the year before to slave in the sugar-beet fields), and having conceived your lecture as part of a plot against the Allied powers. You were summoned by the principal, a good man, now an elderly man, on the verge of apoplexy. Stuttering and spluttering, he threatened you with immediate dismissal. You stood there Paddon in his office and tried to feel unshakable and heroic, impervious to attack, satisfied to know you were on the side of truth and virtue in the face of crass injustice. Yet you could not quite manage to bring it off. You cringed at the mere thought of the look on Karen's face if you had to tell her you'd lost your job. Expostulating and expectorating, the principal upbraided you. You began to feel afraid. Perhaps you had been wrong and genuinely wrong. Perhaps the missionaries had softened a blow which was inevitable. Perhaps without their gentle but persistent efforts at mediation, the Indians' destiny would have been more brutal still. Perhaps some of them actually had been generous and good-hearted. Perhaps their medical knowledge had saved lives. And there was no denying that Albert Lacombe, whom the Blackfoot called Good Heart, had risked his life to put across his message of peace, rushing into the midst of frays between the Blackfoot and the Cree, oblivious to bullets whinging about his ears, speaking to the natives in their own tongues, doing his ardent utmost to preserve their past, painstakingly transcribing their legends and their lore. These ideas were not the principal's — he was holding forth about the school's reputation and how you, Mr. Sterling, were a blot on it, how he had done you a number of favours in the thirties but did not intend to put up much longer with your whims, how this was the last warning and if there were any further complaints or conflicts involving one of your classes he would take great pleasure in giving you the sack if it were the last thing he did before retirement — no, these ideas were opening up inside of you like crevices, danger-ous quake-faults that seemed liable to bring everything you had built with Miranda crashing to the ground.

You walked home in an unprecedented state of anguish.

And, anguished, managed somehow to finish the term. Not a word was ever breathed between you and your students about the Father Lacombe fiasco. In August, while hundreds of your countrymen died assaulting the German fortifications at Dieppe, you dreamed that you were with them, and wounded, and in pain, and Father Lacombe bent over you, the legendary piece of camphor between his teeth, smiled kindly at you with his crinkly blue eyes and whispered Shall you be saved, Paddon? Shall you be saved? — gesturing with his black-sleeved arm to the thousands of corpses overflowing the mass grave he had scraped out in the cold earth with his own hands and smiling at you once more as you thrashed about feverishly until Karen woke you by kissing you with her cool lips.

O Canada Our land our pride our love High be thine aim All self-ish aims above Thy maple leaves blood-red recall Christ's cross of splendid pain Thy golden sheaves made bread for all His life whose death was gain — You buried your face in Miranda's crotch and licked her to kingdom come and then, when she was still floating far away, confessed in a whisper these new fears, these questions and misgivings that were making the solid ground of your convictions shift horribly beneath your feet. Her body tensed up and closed itself off from you, language reappeared in her eyes and flashed anger, she said Nothing was worse than those men of God, no, how can you change your mind when we talked about this so many days, Paddon?

She was truly angry. Damn you, she said, for thinking that and coming here and being with me. How dare you make me happy with something in your head you know would make me mad? She kicked and shoved and you almost felt relieved, thinking Maybe she'll be able to make that ground solid again. Damn you, Paddon, why you just always believe the last person you talk to? I told you the story of Crowfoot. You know about his life, how he was so damn grateful to the Mounties for getting rid of the whisky traders he never dared rise up against the Whites. You know about what a reasonable guy he was, not joining up with Sitting Bull's angry Sioux, not joining up with the Ghost Dancers, not joining up with the Riel Rebellion, always holding back, holding off, telling his people Wait and see, who knows, maybe the Whites keep their word this time after all, and every single time that bastard Lacombe would be there, saying God loved him for turning the other cheek — how goddamn many cheeks is a man supposed to have, Paddon? But what you don't know about is the way he died. Crowfoot could feel it when his death was close by, he made a beautiful farewell speech and went into the great skin house and just lay down. Medicine men from the whole confederacy gathered around for many days and nights, drumming and chanting and dancing the end of his life. He always believed in their powers — you know Paddon, he never learned English, he never once said to Lacombe. You're right and we're wrong, he just always tried to save what could be saved. Finally the hour came. The medicine men sensed it and went away to leave Crowfoot alone with his death. And you know what those asshole priests did? — Miranda's lower lip trembled and as she answered her own question tears of rage sprang to her eyes — They destroyed everything the medicine men prepared! Even in the very last second of his life, they couldn't leave Crowfoot alone! They said their magic words to undo the other magic! They snuck inside the skin house and shoved a fucking wafer down his throat!

Miranda was sobbing now, furious and sobbing, and you realized you had never seen her weep before, and as you waited for her to calm down enough for you to take her in your arms you noticed uneasily that her anger had not quite succeeded in stopping up the gaping gaps inside of you. But she did not calm down at all that afternoon, she was deeply hurt and when the two of you had got out of bed and put your clothes back on in a ghastly silence she told you to leave and so for the first time in six years you separated without a kiss, without the exchange of glances that poured hope into your limbs, without even having decided when you would meet again.

Forever afterwards you would feel responsible for what happened to Miranda the following day, though she repeatedly insisted that it was not the first time, that she had had two previous attacks, one in 1930 and one in 1935, and that indeed (though she had never told you this before and you listened with the nauseous attention of the betrayed) these attacks were what had incited her to paint in the first place.

The early signs were always visual, she said, there was a bizarre modification of her eyesight, a sudden narrowing of her field of vision, and then — a day or two later — the appearance of arcs, rays, vectors which divided the world, thrillingly and frighteningly, into irregular blocks of colour, distorting objects not beyond recognition but beyond belief, and you stared Paddon as she described the glowing blues and the swirling blood reds, and wondered if she was going to die. Doggedly you tried to follow the chain of causes and effects back to where it had begun — her tears of rage, your inner crevices, Lacombe's blue-eyed love, the Haitian conflagrations — but this was not the point, the point was that Miranda had lost all sensation in her right arm her right leg and several patches of her face, and was patiently waiting for it to return while putting up with blinding flashes of light and implosions of inner darkness. And the chain extended back far beyond the day when you had first set eyes on her and fallen in love with the paint in her hair which was, in fact, a symptom.

———•———

And now at last I see it, now at last the details are crowding in on me, now at last I can say how it came about: on the evening of December 31, 1899, in the pretty little frontier town at the junction of the Bow and Elbow rivers, a welcoming parade was held for the returned men from South Africa. It wended its joyful way among the handful of sandstone buildings that formed Calgary's downtown, ending up at the Palliser Hotel for the barracks ball.

The night was clear and icy cold and the moon was full, let's say the moon was full, and shone with such brilliance that the black-dark Rocky Mountains could be made out in the light-dark distance. The Palliser was festooned like a red-white-and-blue wedding cake, draped with miles of bunting and glowing with gas-lit pride. Every white woman respectable or not within a fifty-mile radius had donned her longest frilliest dress, fried her hair into ringlets with curling-irons and blushed pink onto her lips and cheeks. Every white man who had a uniform was wearing it and those who did not had scraped the cow dung from their spurs, shined their high-heeled boots with stove blacking and done their best to spank their jeans and jackets back to spiffiness.

I see Mildred. Young, broad-shouldered, breathless with excitement. The blue taffeta of her one and only evening gown bringing out the subtle hue of her eyes. A family heirloom studded with three South African diamonds dangling into her squarish bodice. I see John. His jaw dropping slightly as he sets eyes on her and his heart skipping a beat. Not only was she taller than he was but she clearly came from a better class, she would probably make fun of his accent the minute he opened his mouth and turn away from him in search of more cultivated company but no, to his astonishment, impressed perhaps by his cavalry uniform, she graciously accepted his invitation to dance.

Oh that dance, Paddon! Oh the happy hopefulness of those couples as they shyly grinned then gaily grabbed each other's waists and started working up a sweat — in the male and female trickles of secret secretions I can feel you already on the verge of entering the world, why this world Paddon, whatever for, just because this flesh is irrigated with hormones and these intrepid new settlers are determined to multiply, it's in the air, a whiff of murky musk that says wow, *There'll be a hot time in the old town tonight.*

God of the prairies by Thy boundless grace Give us the strength to build a worthy race That shall not lose its steadfast faith in Thee Through all the winds and hails of destiny . . . John Sterling had never before held the body of a great lady against his own. His first wife Lizzy had been the mangy scroungy daughter of a prostitute; he and his brother Jake had hired her to cook for the farmhands and he had knocked her up out of thoughtlessness and married her out of guilt — who would have dreamed that after so much tragedy, after that god-awful mess of his gasping wife and his mangled son, he would one day discover *this*? — a tall soft-blue woman smiling at him as he took her in his arms, then spinning round the room with him beneath the sparkling chandeliers as the orchestra waltzed them towards a shimmering mirage of new horizons, then glancing sweetly through her eyelashes at him as he poured her a glass of sparkling champagne that frothed over and down into the frothy lace of her sleeve, then blushing as he dared to kiss her longer than the resounding smacks being exchanged left and right to celebrate the birth of the Twentieth Goddamn Century, Can You Believe It? then growing visibly tipsy and drowsy as he filled her glass and danced with her again, filled her glass and danced with her again, the alcohol bolstering his self-confidence, then letting him drape her dark woollen cloak over her shoulders and leaning against him in the frosty winter night, then returning his kisses with surprising vigour beneath the jaded blank stare of the moon, after all he *was* a military man and she *had* come out here to get hitched, then actually letting his hand graze her blue taffeta breasts until he thought his legs would simply dissolve with lust, then pushing him away as he slipped his other hand beneath her stiff and scratchy swathes of skirt, then letting herself sink into the snowbank after all with a giggle and a sigh, then struggling to get up again as he fell on top of her and the last partiers went past, their words blurred with liquor but their laughter cutting crystal-clear wedges in the night air, then realizing what was happening and coming to her senses when it was very nearly too late, then resisting no longer but putting herself in the hands of God as John Sterling's sinewy fingers undid the buttons of his cavalry breeches and thrust his impatient love-starved self into her just in time.

And God took over from there, distractedly as usual because He had His mind on other things: without so much as clearing His throat he boredly muttered His abracadabra over the greasy matter in Mildred's womb so that a glimmer of spirit would come into it, absently hummed his ancient little refrain about mankind, lethargically dragged you from nothingness, Paddon, against His better judgement and your better interests, then heaved a sigh and, staring off into space, continued drumming His fingers on Eternity.

Acknowledgements

Many people helped me in the writing of this book, wittingly or unwittingly, by their friendship or their knowledge or both. I wish to express my special thanks to Jacques Rey Charlier for the wealth of his wisdom on Haiti and to Denis Hirson for his literary rigour. Emile Martel, former director of the Canadian Cultural Centre in Paris, put many fascinating documents at my disposal, and Ghislaine Simmoneau, unfortunately since deceased, generously facilitated my library research in the same centre. Finally, my brother Lorne Huston, my father James Huston, and my stepmother Maria Huston will never know all the good they have done me.